"An engrossing tale of murder an̶̶ ̶̶ ̶̶ ̶̶ ̶̶, ̶̶ ̶̶ ̶̶ a revealing exploration of the ever-popular locked-room mystery, Mead's debut is a novel to intrigue and delight."

—JOHN CONNOLLY

"This clever mystery combines a delightful homage to Golden Age detective fiction with a highly entertaining impossible crime puzzle—what more could any fan of classic crime wish for?"

—MARTIN EDWARDS

"An absolute delight. The Golden Age of detective fiction comes brilliantly alive. Great characters, wonderful locked-room puzzles, it kept me hooked."

—JIM ELDRIDGE

"Both a splendid homage to the Golden age of impossible crimes and its great exponent John Dickson Carr and a witty reconstruction of the classic locked room mystery with tongue in cheek bravado and a gallery of attendant, endearing characters, Tom Mead's debut is a sheer delight."

—MAXIM JAKUBOWSKI

"A real treat for mystery fans."

—RAGNAR JONASSON

"Mead's debut novel is a valentine to the locked-room puzzles of John Dickson Carr, to whom it is dedicated... Mead faithfully replicates all the loving artifice and teasing engagement of golden-age puzzlers in this superior pastiche."

—KIRKUS

"This debut, a tribute to John Dickson Carr and other Golden Age masters of the locked-room mystery, will appeal to nostalgia buffs and fans of the classics."

—LIBRARY JOURNAL

DEATH
AND THE
CONJUROR

DEATH
AND THE
CONJUROR

TOM MEAD

THE MYSTERIOUS PRESS
NEW YORK

DEATH AND THE CONJUROR

Mysterious Press
An Imprint of Penzler Publishers
58 Warren Street
New York, N.Y. 10007

First Mysterious Press paperback edition: 2023

Interior design by Maria Fernandez

Library of Congress Control Number: 2022902581

ISBN: 978-1-61316-423-5
eBook ISBN: 978-1-61316-319-1

10 9 8 7 6 5 4 3 2 1

Printed in the United States of America
Distributed by W. W. Norton & Company

To my mum and dad
and
To the memory of JDC
(1906–1977)

CONTENTS

PART THREE: THE IMPOSTOR'S TALE

DRAMATIS PERSONAE

Dr. Anselm Rees, a psychologist

Dr. Lidia Rees, his daughter

Floyd Stenhouse, a musician (Patient A)

Della Cookson, an actress (Patient B)

Claude Weaver, a writer (Patient C)

Benjamin Teasel, an impresario

Lucy Levy, an actress

Marcus Bowman, a financier and playboy

Tweedy, a publisher

Pete Hobbs, an elevator boy

Olive Turner, a housekeeper

Assorted maids, clerks and supernumeraries

George Flint, a police inspector

Jerome Hook, a police sergeant

Joseph Spector, a professional trickster

PART ONE
THE THIEF'S TALE

(September 11, 1936)

For the theatre, one needs long arms.

—Sarah Bernhardt, *Memories of My Life*

Friday, September 11, 1936

I

FIERCE STUFF

A t the Pomegranate Theatre, tempers flared like oil lamps. "Have you had my earring?" demanded Lucy Levy. The stagehand simply gaped and did not answer her.

Miss Levy tutted and moved on. She made her way round the whole backstage crew, ducking under beams and bobbing round costume trolleys, batting her dusky grey eyelids and moueing those pink, petulant lips of hers. But there was no sign of the earring.

It was the final run-through of *Miss Death* before opening night, so the atmosphere was taut as piano wire. Miss Levy (second female lead) had been struggling for the last fortnight to retain her composure as the big moment inched nearer. And there was still no sign of the earring.

Lucy strode out from the wings and toward centre stage, heels thumping on bare wood. "Della, if you've pinched my earring . . ."

"*Look out!*" came a voice from the wings. It was Benjamin Teasel. Lucy almost tumbled headfirst through an open trapdoor. She halted at the last moment, her foot poised over the empty air.

"Yes, that could have been quite nasty," said a second voice. Two men emerged from the wings on the opposite side of the stage, Teasel in the green Norfolk suit he wore to establish authority. The other fellow was older, and dressed—somewhat outrageously—in a black cloak lined in crimson silk.

Miss Levy took a moment to catch her breath. She blinked at Teasel, then turned to the other man. "Who are *you?*"

"Lucy, don't be rude," Teasel chided. He liked to play the reproving schoolmaster. "This is Joseph Spector." He said the name as though she ought to know already who the old man was.

"Pleasure." Spector smiled. It was a cadaverous smile. He seemed to belong to a bygone era; his suit—which was black velvet—bore the faded glamour of the prosperous 1890s, and his face was creased like balled-up notepaper. But he had a pair of deep-set eyes of the palest blue she had ever seen.

Though his gait and dress sense were those of a very old man, his voice was gentle and somehow innocent. He looked to Lucy like somebody who could get away with almost any crime.

He explained: "We're just fine-tuning the act three illusion. If you'd be so good as to vacate the stage?" And Lucy

Levy, still breathless and missing an earring, stepped off without a word. But she lingered long enough to hear the two men exchange murmurs.

"My God," Teasel rumbled, "I swear one of these days I'll kill her."

"High spirits is all it is. And besides, if you leave her to her own devices she may do it herself," said Spector, kneeling beside the open trapdoor. "All set down there?" he called.

"Aye-aye, sir!" came the reply.

Spector gave a little smile, then winked at Teasel. "Let's have a look at it, shall we?"

There was a brief pause before a gruesome wax figure emerged silently from the trapdoor. Its ghoulish face peered out into the empty auditorium, its hands contorted into grasping claws.

"Excellent," said Spector, "though we might perhaps tighten up the timing."

"Looked all right to me," Teasel said.

"It has to be *split-second*, Benjamin. I want punters shrieking in their seats. Perhaps a little more grease in the mechanism?"

"No time. We need to get to Della's act two monologue. Where is she?"

Chastened, Joseph Spector headed backstage. From his inside pocket he produced a cigarette case containing ten narrow, black cigarillos. He placed one between his teeth and lit it, exhaling a plume of fragrant smoke into the musty air. Lucy Levy watched from a little shadowed alcove nestled in the maze of backstage corridors. She studied this "Joseph Spector" unseen.

His age was hard to pin down. Depending on the lighting, he looked anywhere from fifty to eighty. Like all conjurors he played up to the confusion. She did not know it, but "Joseph Spector" was not his given name either—it was an alias from another life, from his career as a music hall conjuror. But although he had retired from performing more than a decade before, he'd worked hard to preserve his famous *legerdemain*.

Now he headed for the stage door, where the doorman smiled and, with a jangle of keys, let him out onto the side street. Lucy followed but did not immediately plunge through the door as he had. Instead she looked at the doorman and, with a finger pressed threateningly to her lips, eased the door open a crack and peeped out. Outside she glimpsed Della Cookson, ludicrously perched on a dustbin in full costume.

"Della," said Spector, "what are you doing out here?"

The star smiled at him. "Well I have to go *somewhere*, don't I?"

Even Lucy had to admit that, facially, Della Cookson was a sensation. From her arched black eyebrows to the shadowed dimple in her chin, the merest twitch could evoke a whirlwind of emotions. And with her face framed by a tumble of auburn hair, she might have stepped from a photograph. To call her "larger-than-life" would be a misnomer; she was diminutive, but in her gestures and expressions there was an expansiveness and vibrancy that was almost preternatural.

Like so many artists, though, she was subject to periodic melancholies that incapacitated her—sometimes for weeks at a time—and had given her a reputation. Today she was looking bleak, with the pale skin and crimson lips of a consumptive on the fade.

"Not even opening night," she said, "and already they're crucifying us." She held up a newspaper: TAWDRY SPOOKSHOW was the two-word headline.

"I never thought you'd be the sort to take that kind of thing personally, Della," said Spector.

"Easy for you to say. It's not *you* they're taking potshots at, is it?"

"I'll have you know," the old man went on, "this show is built on *my* tricks and *my* illusions. They're like children to me. I've nurtured them for many, many years."

Della gave him a sad smile and changed the subject. "Just how old *are* you, Joseph? I've been wondering."

"Oh, at least five hundred. I distinctly remember the Spanish Armada. *Ruined* my tenth birthday, it did."

Della laughed politely. "You magicians. You just can't give a straight answer, can you?"

"Certainly not. It's why Teasel hired me. Straight answers are no good to him. Admittedly, *Miss Death* is a lurid tale. And so it requires the most elaborate mise-en-scène known to man. That's what makes it *perfect* for a venue like this. Newly refurbished. All that glorious space to fill. If Benjamin can't pack 'em in with a show like this, nobody can."

"Good old Benjamin Teasel," Della said with ill-concealed venom. "Why's he sent you out here anyway? I'd have thought you were vital to the run-through. All those monsters of yours popping out from under the floorboards."

"Maybe two months ago I was vital. But these days you might say I've become conscious of my own superfluity."

"It must be strange seeing other people performing your tricks."

"'Surreal' might be a better word. But it's not entirely without pleasure. After all, the tricks still work. And that's something, isn't it?"

Della took a sip from a flask. "Care for a dram?"

Spector took it from her. "What's in it?"

She shrugged. "I try not to think about it, actually."

After a beat, Spector's curiosity won out. "Oh, why not?" He took a small sip. The alcohol singed the back of his throat and seared a flaming path down his gullet. He gave a dry, roaring cough. "Fierce stuff," he said.

Della laughed. "Oh, and Joseph? Don't tell any of the others about this, will you? The drinking, I mean. It's just first-night nerves. I'll stop once we get into the run."

Spector smiled at her but didn't answer. He said a quick goodbye and slipped away, leaving the theatre behind him. So close to opening night—mere hours now—they would get by just as well without him. He took a last look at the billboard above the front of house (DELLA COOKSON IN "MISS DEATH") before disappearing amid the blur of roving souls along the Strand. Just another grey speck, collar upturned against the biting autumn air, trudging toward St. Martin-in-the-Fields.

With a sharp-edged smile, Lucy Levy eased shut the stage door.

II

MISS DEATH

T he sky beyond the window of the house in Dollis Hill had turned a monstrous puce. Early evening was casting a pall over London. Dr. Anselm Rees sat at his desk scribbling notes, while Patient A lay on the leather divan at the far side of the room with his gaze fixed on the corniced ceiling. He was telling a story.

"And I can't move, and I'm lying there breathless and paralysed, when all of a sudden there's a pair of eyes watching me from the darkness. And I'm peering around, trying to see, when the door swings open and this dark figure glides into the room and stands there at the foot of my bed."

"The figure—who is he?" Dr. Rees spoke with only the slightest accent.

"My father."

Rees nodded—it was as he had anticipated.

"But he's sort of different, somehow. Like a ghost."

"Your father—I mean your *real* father—he is living?"

"Yes. I haven't seen or spoken to him for a few months, but he's alive and kicking, all right."

"You have no fears or anxieties concerning his health?"

"Nothing I can put my finger on. But in the dream he's there at the foot of my bed, staring down at me with unblinking eyes. He's wearing a kind of robe, like a monk's habit. I feel almost as if I'm lying on a sacrificial altar, as though I'm about to be slaughtered as an offering to some pagan god."

"And then?"

"And then he reaches up and tears at the robe, exposing his bare chest. And I"—patient A paused for a moment, collecting himself. This was a very difficult story for him to tell—"and I see for the first time what has happened to him."

Dr. Rees studied his patient expectantly, his pen nib hovering over the page.

The younger man continued: "His rib cage has become . . . a mouth. His chest opens up like a pair of jaws and I can see a set of gleaming, razor-sharp teeth. And from deep in his chest, where his heart should be, I can see . . . a tongue."

Patient A ceased his monologue, tears welling in his eyes.

"Is that the end of the dream?" Rees persisted.

"No. No, it's not the end. But I don't think I can tell you any more now."

"I understand. Let's terminate the session here. But I have some theories on the symbolic nature of this dream."

"*Father!*"

Patient A sprang to his feet. "Who's that?" he yelped. "Who's calling?"

"It's only my daughter, Lidia," said Doctor Rees. "She's upstairs." He strode over to the door and flung it open before calling out into the hall: "What is it, Lidia?"

"Marcus is here," came the reply. "His car just rounded the corner."

"Ah," said the doctor, turning back to his patient. "Then please call me tomorrow and we will resume our discussion. In the meantime, I shall write you another prescription for Veronal."

"I haven't met your daughter," said Patient A absently.

"No. She's not currently seeing patients. But she possesses a formidable psychiatric insight, and she is working on a series of articles for the *New Statesman*," Rees said, leaning over the desk and scribbling out the prescription on his pad. He tore off the sheet and handed it to the younger man.

"If it's not too much trouble," ventured Patient A, "I'll leave by the French windows."

"Of course," said Rees. "I understand you want our meetings to be confidential. Here, let me." And with that, the elderly doctor strode over to the French windows and produced a key from his smoking jacket. He unlocked the windows and let his patient out into the garden. Beyond the narrow overhang of grey stone was the hard soil of a stark flowerbed.

Patient A was not as young as he looked. There was a certain world-weariness around his pale eyes. He was clean-shaven, and dressed in a slipshod fashion: an ill-fitting tweed suit that bulged over his belly. He was by trade a musician, one of the finest violinists the Philharmonic had ever known. And his real name (for it must be broached eventually) was Floyd Stenhouse. But Floyd took his troubled dreams and his prescription and scuttled away through the garden and out the back gate.

There was something a little off about his gait as he strode away along Dollis Hill Road. Of course, anybody glimpsing him in passing would take him for one of those delightful English eccentrics with so much character in his face and intelligence deep in those close-set eyes. But the real reason for the slightly off-kilter walk was a weight in the pocket of his trench coat. With his hand buried in the pocket, he felt the cold grip of the handle. It was a war souvenir, a gift from his uncle. A revolver.

Dollis Hill itself was an affluent suburb of wide, meandering streets lined by Edwardian houses and lush hedgerows. The Rees place was built from sturdy redbrick, its Italianate frontage framed by ornate stone quoins and studded with three rows of white-framed sash windows. The front door was up a sweep of stone steps from the street. It was not all that dissimilar to the home Dr. Rees had left behind in Vienna.

Anselm Rees had set up shop here in North West London as soon as he arrived in the country five months before. He had spent his whole life up to that point in Vienna, but for reasons both personal and political he had made the painful decision to emigrate. He was an old man now, with a throbbing toothache and fading eyesight. But his brain remained as sharp as a pin, his wit as quick, and his celebrated dress sense as effortlessly chic. It had not taken him long to find his niche in London high society. When he disembarked from HMS *Magnificent* at the Southampton docks in late February, he sported a top hat and tailcoat. He strode down the gangplank, arm in arm with the one creature on Earth he valued above himself: his daughter, Lidia.

Flashbulbs had flared that day as father and daughter descended onto English terra firma. Lidia was good for the photos, with her arch, jaw-level, jet-black bob and her modish fashions—her neck hung with beads, and a particular penchant for mannish tweeds offset by furs. Her face was smooth-skinned, with the piquant features of a Louise Brooks. But her voice was soft and accented with languid rolling syllables.

Rees himself was no slouch either when it came to charming the natives. He'd made it clear that he had no intention of taking on any new patients. It was barely a month before he reneged on this pledge. In fact, he took on three patients: two male, one female. Their identities were kept in the strictest confidence—tabloids would have paid a lot of money for that information. In his notebooks he referred to them only as Patients A, B, and C. But of course, Lidia knew who they were even if she did not meet them. And it is important to state that she never breathed a word.

Dr. Rees closed and locked the window. Save for the faint odour of terror-sweat, it was as if he had received no visitor at all. As he turned away from the glass, he was startled to find Lidia standing in the doorway, hands on hips.

The study was at the very rear of the house; a vast, square high-ceilinged room, lit by crystal chandeliers, carpeted with Turkish rugs, and lined with shelves of leather-bound volumes:

multilingual classics and specialist medical texts, all in pristine editions. The room was austere, yet at the same time there was a musty homeliness to it, as though it were lived in without actually being lived in. Its features were a varnished Biedermeier writing desk, a divan-style sofa piled with velvet pillows (for the patients), and the grey stone fireplace. In the far corner stood a large teakwood packing trunk. Wherever you looked in the room, the trunk was a constant presence on the periphery of your vision. It loomed there, coffin-like and faintly sinister.

"You're not dressed," said Lidia.

"But I am."

"Not for the theatre you're not."

Anselm Rees sighed. "I'd completely forgotten."

"Well, you had better make it quick. Marcus is here and we're setting off in fifteen minutes—with or without you."

It was a close call but they made it. Anselm Rees stumped down the stairs in his evening wear, straightening his bow tie, with just a minute to spare.

"Good evening to you, sir," said Marcus Bowman.

Anselm Rees looked the young man up and down. The fellow was tall and spindly, rather spiderish in a pin-striped suit and garish red bow tie. He had a film-star moustache and slick, brilliantined black hair. His eyes were as damp and unintelligent as a dog's.

This unlikely trio headed out to Bowman's car—an Austin landaulet in bumblebee yellow—and set off for the Pomegranate.

While they drove, Dr. Rees studied the couple in the bench seat beside him. They were a mismatched pair. Lidia was, of course, very beautiful, but she was a firebrand and an intellectual. Marcus Bowman came from a long line of financiers and had gone to one of the finer public schools, but he was as vapid and vacuous as a half-pumped balloon. He drove his car like a tearaway and dressed like some sort of playboy. Dr. Rees found it difficult to look on this fellow with anything but contempt.

Lidia was hellishly quick to adapt to her new surroundings. At twenty-six she had just completed her own doctorate in psychology. However, her theories diverged from her father's at intriguing junctures. You might even say there existed a professional rivalry between them. But Lidia knew how to have a good time as well. She ventured boldly and unchaperoned into some of London's most stylish nightclubs, where her beauty and mysterious, continental manner drew considerable attention. One of her favourites was the Palmyra Club in Soho, where the drink was cheap and the jazz almost unbearably boisterous. And it was there that she'd first met Marcus Bowman, the man who would shortly become her fiancé.

Marcus Bowman was a Bright Young Thing with a faint overbite—especially prominent squirrelish molars—and a bulbous Adam's apple that gave him the humorous look of an undersketched *Punch* cartoon. He dressed like the *bon viveur* he was, with plus fours and typically with a golf bag draped over a shoulder. Not to mention the moustache—which had once been the subject of a *Top-Storey Chap* puff piece on male grooming—and seemed to drowse lazily on his upper lip, just as he himself tended to drape himself over furniture rather than sit in it. When he spoke it was in the scarcely comprehensible plummy argot of the in-bred English bourgeois, every sentence punctuated by a "what-what" or an "I say!"

And yet, Marcus seemed to make Lidia happy . . .

The streets hummed with vespertine anticipation as theatregoers gathered outside the Pomegranate for the opening night. Marcus parked the car and the trio clambered out. Anselm read *Miss Death*, the play's title, on the billboard with a sigh. The doors of the theatre were flung wide. The foyer was crammed with chattering crowds, clinking glasses and skimming programmes. Anselm was in no mood to socialise and made sullenly for his seat. Lidia went with him while Marcus went to buy some cigarettes from the concession stand.

"What is it, Papa? You seem out of sorts."

"Oh, I'm all right," said the old man. "Just tired."

"Of what?" asked his daughter.

"I think it was Dr. Johnson who said, 'The man who is tired of London is tired of life.' Does that answer your question?" he said, returning her half smile.

At that point an old man in a silk-lined cloak, looking like some penny-dreadful evildoer, excused himself and slid past them along the row. Rees studied the fellow for a moment before returning his attention to the stage.

He checked his watch. Perhaps five minutes to curtain up.

"So who is this Helen Cookson anyway?" asked Marcus.

"*Della* Cookson," Lidia corrected him. "She's one of the greatest actresses of the age. Don't be such a philistine, Marcus."

And with that, the curtain rose.

Act one came and went. Lucy Levy was a vivacious presence, and Della held the audience rapt from her first appearance. Even the sullen old Dr. Rees sat forward in his seat when she arrived onstage. A brief intermission preceded act two, and then the ante was upped. There were more shocks and more laughs, and the cloaked fellow beside them seemed particularly delighted with some of the onstage effects.

The intermission between acts two and three was lengthier, so Rees ventured out into the bar. No sooner had he stepped out than a voice from behind him said his name.

"You'll forgive me for prying, but are you Dr. Anselm Rees?"

Rees turned. "I am. How may I be of service?"

"Teasel's the name. Benjamin Teasel. I'm the producer and director of this little Grand Guignol." The impresario was resplendent in black tie, and he snared in his faintly quivering fist a martini.

"Then I must congratulate you. Your work is having a profound effect on the audience."

"Very kind, thank you." The man inclined his head with calculated modesty. "I hope I'm not intruding, but I wanted to extend an invitation to you and your daughter."

"Oh?"

"Tomorrow night. A party at my place in Hampstead. I thought I'd wait until the reviews were in—that's why I'm having the shindig *tomorrow* night," he explained.

"You're optimistic, then?"

Teasel gave a chuckle. "Just look around you, Doctor! Look at that sea of smiling, chattering faces. *That*, my friend, is the audience of a show that is going to run and run. But I want to wait until the notices are saying so too. Then I'll be able to enjoy drinks and music without that overhanging dread of tomorrow's papers . . ."

"I see. An interesting proposition, but I'm afraid I have plans for tomorrow night.'

"Really? Oh, such a shame. I should have loved to hear a psychiatrist's interpretation of this diabolical little drama. Well, take my card anyway, won't you, in case you change your mind. Oh, Edgar! Edgar Simmons!" Teasel's attention had been caught by another guest. "Edgar, where *have* you been hiding yourself these past few months . . . ?" And the producer drifted away on the sea of admirers.

Rees was not averse to the occasional soirée—it was an inevitable hive of potential patients, after all. But something about Teasel had rubbed him the wrong way. The very air around him smacked of showbiz sleaze. Rees gave a little shudder and returned to the auditorium.

He made it back to his seat just in time for the act three curtain.

"Who was that you were talking to?" Lidia wanted to know.

"Benjamin Teasel. He directed this . . . extravaganza. Wants me to go to a party tomorrow night."

"Good God. There's no escaping them, is there? Parasites."

At the mention of Teasel's name, the man in the cloak's ears pricked up. He now seemed on the verge of butting in on the Rees family confab. But then the curtain rose.

The third act was the one in which all the disparate features of the play finally coalesced. There was a particularly ghoulish trapdoor trick that caught even the doctor off guard. The audience gasped. The final curtain fell, and the applause was instantaneous and affectionate. A few even sprang to their feet as Della Cookson emerged for her curtain call.

Della strode forward beneath a spotlight, took her bow, and was presented with a lavish bouquet by an admirer in the front row. She stood with tears gleaming in her eyes as she lapped up the audience adulation. She had a way about her, as portraits are said to do, of making it seem as though she were making eye contact with each audience member individually. But this was wishful thinking—in fact there was only one man she was looking at that evening, whose face she had picked out instantly. Dr. Anselm Rees.

On his way out, an usher slipped him a note. The audience members around him were filing back into the foyer and the bar, chattering amiably about the night's entertainment. Rees stopped and unfolded the paper.

"Go on without me," he said to Marcus and Lidia.

"But how will you get home?"

"I'll take a cab. Don't worry about me." And he slipped away through the crowd.

Another usher was on hand to escort him behind the bar and through to the backstage area. "This way sir," she said, holding open the door for him.

Rees stepped through and found himself in another world. Stagehands were celebrating, and the stage manager was flipping through a tattered copy of the script making swift and brutal amendments with a stubby pencil. Rees followed the usher down a lengthy corridor toward the star dressing room. They knocked on the door.

"Just a moment," said a voice from within.

Rees waited.

Then the door was opened by the star of the show, Della Cookson. But to Dr. Rees, she was Patient B.

She was beaming and luminous in her greeting, favouring him with an affectionate peck on the cheek. She bade him sit in her chair in front of the makeup mirror, before slamming the door in the usher's face.

"So what did you think of the show, Doctor?"

"My daughter is an admirer of thrillers," he said awkwardly, meeting her glance in the mirror. "Oh—you appear to have dropped something, Della."

"Where?"

Rees pointed at something gleaming on the carpet. "There. What is it?" He leaned over to retrieve the item. "Just some jewellery." He handed it to Della, who slipped it into the pocket of her kimono. It was a single gold earring.

Della settled down and began removing her makeup.

"Why did you ask me here tonight, Della?"

Patient B sighed and studied herself in the mirror. Then, slowly, she turned to him. "Because, Doctor, I've done something very terrible."

PART TWO
THE LIAR'S TALE

(September 12–14, 1936)

In magic, today as always, the effect is what counts. The method or methods used are always purely secondary.

—Dai Vernon

Most people, I am delighted to say, are fond of the locked room. But—here's the damned rub—even its friends are often dubious.

—John Dickson Carr, *The Hollow Man*

ENTR'ACTE (I)

THE MAN IN THE LONG BLACK COAT

Saturday, September 12, 1936

L ike the poverty-stricken artists of revolutionary Paris, Claude Weaver tended to write his novels in an attic.

The attic in question nestled above his two-storey Hampstead home; it had been modified to accommodate bookshelves and his writing desk. His wife often made the hyperbolic claim that he seldom came out of his attic, that he preferred its company to hers. This was mostly untrue. He frequently came out—he just preferred that she did not notice him.

Weaver was by nature an inconsequential man, the sort who might be passed in the street without as much as a second glance. If you were to meet him you would find him quiet, subdued, even shy. He *never* gave interviews. He *never* showed his face at literary luncheons or benefit evenings.

With this in mind, his wife, Rosemary, now seemed determined to thrust him out of his comfortable cocoon and into the daylight. She was a clever woman, and often inscrutable. But she failed to understand that his solitude was a vital component of his creativity. That was how all the problems had started.

Now, on the morning of September 12, he sat as usual at the desk in his attic, with a typewriter and heap of crisp white paper in front of him. Something was amiss. Today, the words would not come. He had an appointment before lunch, but he had decided to get a couple of hours' writing in beforehand.

This was proving more difficult than anticipated. Something was distracting him. He stood, stretched his aching limbs, and paced around the attic. There was a small round picture window that cast a narrow shaft of light onto the desk. But it also gave him a decent view of the street. He strode over to the window. Almost pressing his nose against the glass, he peered out. It was then that he saw the man in the black coat.

How long had it been? Perhaps a week. A week since Weaver had first become conscious of that undefinable presence. Of *something* pursuing him. Now his waking hours were consumed by an almost supernatural sense of overhanging dread. He thought of Maupassant's "Horla" and for the first time began to wonder if he was truly losing his mind. His paranoia was such that Rosemary was beginning to notice. And that was something he could not permit. Until now he had managed to keep it contained. But on the morning of the twelfth he happened to glance out of the window of his attic, and for the first time he spotted the man in the black coat.

There was little else to say of this fellow, except that he was a man. He stood stock-still on the pavement across the street, looking up at the window. But he wore a lengthy overcoat, and the upper half of his face was shadowed by the wide brim of his hat. All Weaver could make out was that he was clean-shaven.

Weaver thundered down two flights of stairs and flung open the front door. He did not know what he would do if the man was there to meet him; he had not thought that far ahead. Perhaps he nurtured some misguided notion of confronting the fellow, of facing his fear. But the street was empty. The man was gone.

Claude Weaver eased shut the door, sealing himself in with the dirt-coloured leaves that had been carried in with the autumn chill.

III

THREE TELEPHONE CALLS

At Dollis Hill, the day began with a telephone call. Anselm Rees, who had risen late, was at his desk and snatched up the receiver.

"Dr. Rees?"

He recognised the voice on the telephone as belonging to Patient C, who in his daily life was a novelist of some sort. Claude Weaver was the fellow's real name. Rees had made a point of not seeking out his work.

"Mr. Weaver," said Rees, his voice threaded with impatience, "you seem to have missed this morning's appointment."

"I'm sorry. Something came up. I won't be able to make it. I'll pay for the session, of course. But I can't come and see you today."

"Is there a reason for this?"

"I'm sorry." And with that, Patient C hung up the phone. Rees, shaking his head and muttering to himself, reached for his appointment book, flipped through to today's date. He found the name "PATIENT C" and sliced a line through it with his fountain pen.

"Mrs. Turner," he called out, "this morning's appointment has cancelled on me. What shall I do to occupy my time?"

The housekeeper bustled into the study with a tray of tea things. Olive Turner had been housekeeper at the Rees home from the day they first set foot across the threshold. She was a meticulous woman, perceived by some as humourless. Dr. Rees nevertheless observed in her an understated affection and wit that charmed him. Needless to say, she was also very skilled at her job. The house was kept in perfect order, the food cooked to perfection.

"*Article*," she said with mock severity. The article in question was one he was supposedly writing for an esteemed psychiatric journal. An article that even its author found to be as dull as a butter knife. It was hard for him to focus when his three patients were proving to be such fascinating case studies in themselves.

Rees grinned at Olive. "You know I value your concision, Mrs. Turner. It's why I hired you. No superfluous verbiage."

Olive Turner gave him a thin smile. "Well, you asked."

At that moment, the brief silence was splintered once again by the jangle of the telephone. Mrs. Turner laid out the tea things on the small glass-topped table in the centre of the room while the doctor took the call. "Rees here. Who is calling?"

Over the clink of the crockery, Olive could make out a fuzzy voice on the other end of the line. But that was all.

"I see," said Rees into the phone. "Can you tell me more?"

More of that same fuzzy locution. Olive, no longer masking her curiosity, stood up straight to listen.

"I see," the doctor repeated, glancing toward the French windows, "that sounds . . . problematic." Another, lengthier pause. "Yes," the doctor said with a note of finality, "I'll be waiting." And he hung up the phone.

Olive Turner was to recall that second telephone conversation later that night, and to regret that she had let her good manners get in the way of a story. Like so many half-heard and half-remembered conversations, the second call was to prove pivotal.

Lidia Rees let out a yelp. Turning the sheaf of the leather-bound *Die Elixiere des Teufels*, the corner of the page had sliced her thumb and evinced a burble of blood. It dripped onto the page. She sucked on her thumb, trying hard to blink away the pain and focus on the print. But it was too late. Her concentration was broken.

With a groan she slammed shut the book and returned it to her shelf. She was at work in her room on the second floor. Today was a day she had designated for study. Soon she would be launching her own psychiatric practice, and already she was thinking very seriously about generating a list of desirable patients.

She had consciously sought out the niches of London high society. Purely as an observer, you understand. In her eyes the phenomenon of the English upper class presented a fascinating cultural dichotomy. The elders of the set, like those of some Palaeolithic tribe, were models of an arbitrary sense of social propriety. But a brutal war had cracked the façade of security that had enmeshed them for so very long. The boundaries between the classes were being systematically disassembled. And that veneer of propriety was chipping away.

Regardless of class, the younger generation (those who came of age during or after the Great War) was developing a penchant for anarchism. In their politics, of course—the socialist tide was on the surge—but also in their approach to the arts, to music, to everything.

This was the route Lidia's theories were taking. She had already sketched out the outline for an article tentatively titled "The Theory of the English." Was that, she wondered, too sweeping and pompous a title? She would know more when she had started work on her first patient, her first *real* patient.

Her reverie ended abruptly with a rap on her bedroom door.

"Come in," she called out, still sucking on her thumb.

It was Olive Turner. "Telephone call for you downstairs, Miss Rees."

"Funny," said Lidia, "I didn't hear it ring."

"It hasn't stopped all morning, Miss." Despite numerous requests, the housekeeper could not quite bring herself to refer to the young mistress as "Lidia."

"Well, who is it, then?"

"Mr. Marcus Bowman."

Lidia sighed. "Tell him I can't speak to him. Better yet, tell him I'm out."

"I think he's calling to confirm the time for him to pick you up this evening. You're still intending to go with him, I take it?"

Marcus had managed to reserve the couple a table at the Savoy. He had long been promising to treat Lidia to the finest London cuisine, but frequent golfing engagements seemed to scupper his plans. Now at long last the booking was made, and the date set.

"Oh yes. I suppose I'll go with him tonight." She then took a faintly predatory step toward the housekeeper. "Tell him I'll go with him. He can pick me up at eight. Please tell him not to be late."

Lidia gave a little smile. It was a smile that Olive Turner would remember the following day, and she would wonder what it had meant.

IV

THE NIGHT IN QUESTION

"**M**arcus," Lidia greeted her beau with a smile that was becoming and predatory.

"Ahoy there," he said, leaning across the threshold and favouring her with a chaste peck on the cheek. It was only early evening—not yet eight o'clock—but already the sky was the colour of bruised fruit, low and oppressive. Lidia wore a satin evening gown and draped about her neck a ruby necklace. The jewel nestled between her collarbones and gleamed in the light of the street lamps.

"I would invite you in," Lidia said, "but Mrs. Turner's in the middle of cleaning the house. I don't think she'd appreciate it." This was a lie: Olive Turner had finished her cleaning several hours previously. She was now in the kitchen, hard at work on the doctor's dinner.

Lidia stepped out into the street and was about to pull the door shut behind her when Anselm Rees appeared in the hallway, looming behind her left shoulder. "Good evening, Marcus," he said.

"Good evening, sir."

"We'll be late for dinner, Father," said Lidia with forced casualness. "Marcus is going to drive us into town."

"Actually," said Marcus, "I thought we could get a cab. Leave my car here. That way we can make more of a night of it."

"Whatever you want, darling." She slipped her hand into the crook of Marcus's arm and let him lead her toward the roadside. With his free arm he hailed a passing taxi. Anselm Rees stood in the doorway watching as the young couple clambered in and roared off into the evening.

Once they were out of sight, Dr. Rees returned to the dining room, where he sat alone at the table and sipped a drop of sherry.

"Acting funny, isn't she?" said Olive, placing in front of him a dish of steaming beef stew.

"She is my daughter," said Dr. Rees. "How else would you expect her to act?" He said it with humour, but there was truth there too.

At nine p.m. precisely, Olive brought him his supper. By then he had retreated to his study, and when the housekeeper tapped on the door he answered: "Wait a moment."

She heard him clamber from the chair and shuffle in her direction, then twist the key in the lock and pull open the heavy mahogany door. There was a slight furrow in his brow, as of a troubled mind, but apart from that there was nothing in his behaviour to disquiet her.

She handed him the cheeseboard (he stood stolidly in the doorway and evidently did not want her to come in), and he thanked her. Then he told her he had a favour to ask. "Olive, I'm going to be receiving a visitor later this evening. He'll most likely come to the front door, so I don't want you to be alarmed when he arrives. Just let him in, and direct him to the study."

"You don't want me to show him in myself, sir?"

"No." This was a firm instruction—one of the few Anselm Rees ever gave her. "Just let him in, and tell him where to find me. Then go to bed."

Olive opened her mouth to pose another question, but Rees retreated with the cheeseboard and pushed the door shut in her face. The lock clicked noisily into place. Slightly affronted, she returned to the kitchen.

Two hours later—eleven on the nose—pitiful autumn rain began spattering the window. Olive still sat in the kitchen, wrapped in her dressing gown and sipping a mug of cocoa as she read the newspaper by gaslight. And the evening inched along slowly.

Not long after the clock chimed eleven fifteen, there came a rapping at the front door, jolting Olive from a doze. She clambered to her feet and trudged out from the kitchen to the hallway, where she saw a figure silhouetted against the frosted glass. Feeling a sudden pang of fear, she placed the door on the chain before easing it open slightly to get a look at the visitor.

"Yes?" she said, scarcely above a whisper.

"May I come in?" said the man. He wore a trilby pulled down low over his forehead, while his neck and chin were bound up by a thick scarf, muffling his speech. There was little else Olive could discern in the way of detail.

"Who's calling?"

"I'm here to see Dr. Rees."

Olive gritted her teeth, and remembered the doctor's instruction. Reluctantly, she removed the chain from the door and admitted him into the hallway.

"Take your hat and coat, sir?"

"No, thank you," said the man, his voice low and husky. He headed immediately for the staircase.

"Sir!" Olive protested. "If you're looking for Dr. Rees, his office is down the corridor there, the far door on the right."

The stranger halted, and cast an impatient glance in her direction before striding off the way she had indicated. Olive stood watching as the stranger reached the study door, rapped squarely on the wood, and was swiftly admitted.

After a moment, Olive could not contain her curiosity. She crept along the hallway toward the study. Of course it was locked, and the key was in the keyhole, but she could not resist pressing her ear to the wood for a few seconds.

"You don't seem surprised to see me," said the stranger's voice.

"Not at all," came the response from the doctor—his voice was a little low, evidently muffled by the wood. "I've been expecting you."

"Really?" There followed a brief yet troubling silence. Any speech was occluded by the thundering of Olive's heart.

Then the stranger spoke again: "Your housekeeper is spying on us."

Olive felt she might die there in that hallway—the surge of adrenaline and stab of horror in her chest could well prove lethal. Choking back a gasp, she scuttled away.

It took a tot of brandy to calm herself down. Her heart still pounded as she sat alone in the kitchen. There was something very disconcerting about this stranger. Meanwhile, the rain persisted, pelting the glass, creating a propulsive rhythm like tribal drums.

Olive's ears pricked at the sound of the study door unlocking, and of the stranger leaving. It was around half an hour since he arrived. Easing open the kitchen door, she observed through the sliver of space as the stranger—once again bundled in his hat, scarf, and coat—made for the front door. Her inclination was to step out after him, to say, *I'll see you out, sir*, but she couldn't bring herself to do it.

She crept along the corridor so she could see as the stranger pulled open the front door and stepped out into the street. The door swung shut behind him. She watched as his silhouette receded and he disappeared from view. Then she darted from her hiding place and double-bolted the front door.

Next, she headed for the doctor's study. She rapped on the wood and called out: "Everything all right in there, sir?"

"Fine, fine," came the response. It was a little too hasty for Olive's liking.

"You sure about that, sir? You want me to bring you anything? A nightcap?"

"No, thank you. That will be all."

Olive stood for a moment. Then she broached the subject. "May I inquire as to who was visiting you this evening, sir?"

There followed a pause. Olive could hear breathing on the other side of the wood. "Just an old friend," he said, scarcely above a whisper. "Good night."

Olive turned to go. Now, she decided, she really *would* retire to bed. As she made her way toward the staircase, the ghostly silence of the house and the percussive rattle of the rain was shattered by the jangle of the telephone. Olive yelped in fright, stopping in her tracks. She headed for the one that hung from the wall in the hallway but reached it too late. The ringing had already ceased.

She heard the doctor picking up the extension in the study and growling in a scarcely recognisable voice: "What is it?"

There was a pause.

"I see." His tone softened. "And then?"

Olive resumed her position at the study door, her ear pressed to the cold wood. She heard the familiar scratching of the doctor's pen on his notepad. He was taking a few hasty notes. She was almost tempted to pick up the hall extension and listen in on the conversation. But of course that sort of behaviour would be truly beyond the pale.

"Good, this is good," the doctor said. "But now you'd better get some sleep. Really, it's too late to discuss this. Come and see me tomorrow. Ten o'clock. We can go into more detail then. All right. Good night."

And he hung up the phone.

Olive made her way once more to the staircase. As she mounted the first step, she remembered that she had left her book behind on the kitchen table. With a sigh, she turned back.

Eventually, book in hand, she made her way one last time along the hallway toward the staircase.

"Oh lord!" she exclaimed, startled, and loosed her grip on the book. It smacked the tiled floor.

A silhouette stood framed in the frosted glass, tapping gently on the front door. A second visitor?

"Who's that?" she called out.

"Let me in!" came the response. The voice was female.

"Who *is* that?" Olive persisted.

"It's raining! Please let me in!"

Olive crept toward the door and, with a quaking hand, reached out and eased the bolt into its housing. She then heaved open the door and the woman spilled into the house. It was the actress, Della Cookson.

"Thank God," Della breathed.

"Miss Cookson! What do you want at this hour?"

"I need to see Dr. Rees. Please, it's an emergency."

Olive stood for a moment, hands on hips, tapping her foot. "Well, I'll see what I can do. But I'm promising nothing. I happen to know the doctor is still at work in his study. But he never normally sees patients this late. You'd better come through."

She led the way toward the study, halting at the door and balling her fist to knock once again. She gave three strident raps.

They waited.

"Dr. Rees!" Olive called out. "Visitor!"

Della Cookson's shoulders heaved with frantic breaths. Apart from the rain, this was the only sound. Olive pressed her ear once again to the wood.

"Dr. Rees?" she said again.

"Please," said Della, "I have to see him. It's imperative."

Olive pounded on the door. Then she knelt and peered through the keyhole, but of course the view was obstructed by that pesky key. She leaned forward, so that her nose was almost touching the tiled floor, and tried to peer under the door. All she could make out was the thinnest sliver of light. "Something's wrong," she said.

Olive left Della alone in the hall and scuttled to the kitchen. She returned scarcely half a minute later with a pencil and a sheaf of paper. It was an old trick, one so hoary it scarcely requires elucidating in these pages. She slipped the paper under the door, and the pencil she eased into the keyhole. She listened for the thump as the key tumbled out on the other side, before withdrawing the paper and retrieving the key. A neat little sleight of hand, and one that she knew well from her perusals of cheap pulp fiction.

She struggled to her feet, unlocked the door, and plunged in with Della close behind. To begin with, there was nothing apparently untoward within the room. The lights blazed, and the desk was scattered with papers. The doctor's chair was positioned toward the windows, and the man himself lay slumped upon it.

Olive stepped in front of him. She looked at his face. Her heart thundered so loud she barely heard Della scream.

Dr. Anselm Rees lay on that chair freshly dead, his face a white mask and his throat cleaved by a hideous crimson gash. The blood had spilled down his front like a bib. His eyes were half-open and sleepy, while his hands were patiently folded in his lap.

"Close the door," said Olive.

"What?" stammered Della.

"The door! I don't want his daughter to come home and see him like this."

Della did as she was told, pushing shut the study door and sealing them in with the corpse. Olive already had the phone in her hand. "Two three one, Dollis Hill," she announced. "Dr. Anselm Rees has been murdered."

While she provided a few scant details, she looked around the room and noticed something.

"The windows are locked," she said as she hung up the phone.

"Mm?" Della sounded startled.

"The windows. They're locked on the inside." To prove this, she gripped one of the handles and rattled it. It would not move, and the key protruded from the lock.

"So?"

"Then how did the killer get away?"

"What do you mean?"

"He can't have come out through the hall. I was there the whole time. And not five minutes ago—not *five minutes*—I can tell you that the doctor was alive and well in this room because I heard him talking on the telephone."

Della thought about this. "It can't be locked." She reached out and tried the handle for herself. But the windows did not budge.

"It's locked on the inside," said Olive, "just like the door."

Della turned and looked at the corpse. He had sunk down in the chair like an unmanned hand puppet.

In the far corner of the room lay the wooden trunk. Olive caught Della's eye and nodded toward it. Della frowned incredulously. Olive shrugged, as if to say, *Where else would he be?*

The two women crept across the soft plush carpet toward the trunk. Olive looked at Della and held a finger to her lips. She seized the poker from the fireplace and raised it above her head. Then she gave Della a quick nod.

Della leaned forward and wrenched open the trunk.

Olive let fly a fierce war cry and swung the poker like a tennis racquet. But all she hit was empty air. The two women peered inside the trunk. It was perfectly empty.

"Well then, where is he?" demanded Della.

Olive let the poker fall from her grip. It thumped to the carpet. "I, I don't know," she answered.

"I need a drink," Della said.

Olive did not reply.

"No, I mean it. I really need a drink."

"There's sherry on the bureau," said Olive absently.

"Nothing stronger?"

"There's brandy in the kitchen."

"Show me," said Della. "I need to get out of this room."

Olive conceded. "Maybe you're right. We can't do any good here."

The two women went out of the room and Olive led the way to the kitchen—but not before pulling shut the study door behind her, sealing in the late Dr. Rees once again.

They both felt slightly better after a tot of brandy. No less horrified, but more prepared to deal with the practicalities of the situation.

"What I don't understand," Della said, "is where the killer could have gone."

"Nowhere," said Olive. "There was nowhere for him to go."

V

EL NACIMIENTO

The rain had eased to a moribund dribble by the time Inspector George Flint arrived at the Rees house. He was shown through to the murder room, where Anselm Rees was still in his chair, looking increasingly like a half-melted candle.

"A real mess," said Flint to no one in particular. It was true: Rees's head had been half severed at a single stroke. But that expression of calm on his dead face was enough to haunt the nightmares of even a battle-scarred old dog like Flint.

Flint's attitude to crime was philosophical; while largely against it, he could still see it as a societal necessity. Take murder, for instance. Most murders are sordid back-street affairs, no mystery or magic to them. Usually the culprit is whoever was closest to the victim. But increasingly over the last few years, he had been conscious of a burgeoning subgenre of crime, which had rolled over the city like fog. These were the "impossible" crimes—typically high-society affairs, where men in locked rooms were killed under impractical circumstances, or where, for example, a body was found strangled in a snowy field, with only a single set of footprints trailing backward from the corpse. Murder as a puzzle.

It's hard to let oneself become emotionally involved in a case like that. You must retain a sense of intellectual distance. To solve a crime of that variety you need a special sort of brain, which Flint simply did not possess. And so it becomes essential to look elsewhere for your answers.

"Any sign of a weapon?"

"No," answered Jerome Hook. He was Flint's second, a gangly young man well suited to leg work.

"So the killer took it with him. Or else he hid it somewhere in this room. Any joy in tracking down the mysterious visitor from earlier in the evening? The one who put the wind up Mrs. Turner?"

"Not yet. We've got uniforms on the case."

"Good. Let me know as soon as you have anything. And what about this room? Don't tell me we're dealing with any of that 'hermetically sealed' nonsense."

"Afraid so, sir. Both Olive Turner and Della Cookson confirmed the study door was locked on the inside. And as you can see for yourself, the French window is locked on the inside too."

"But the killer *must* have got out that way. If he'd gone through the doorway into the hall then Olive would have seen him, that's fair enough. But it means he *must* have gone via the windows, and then used some trickery to lock them from outside."

"Not possible, I'm afraid, sir. You see, it had been raining for a while at the time of the murder. And just beyond the window is a stretch of flowerbed leading onto the lawn. The water has turned it virtually into slush. So no one could have got away via that route without leaving footprints. And as you can see, there aren't any."

There *were* footprints in the garden—men's footprints—but they did not go anywhere near the house nor the French windows. So someone had been in the garden that night, during the rainstorm. But whoever it might have been, it was impossible to tell if it had occurred before, during, or after the murder. It might even have been a clumsy constable rooting around. Stranger things had happened.

"I see." Flint steepled his fingers and considered the corpse. "So we have a killer who vanished like a ghost. Are we absolutely *convinced* that Rees was alive when the mystery man left?"

"Yes. He called out to Olive through the door. And he was heard taking a telephone call."

"So the murder occurred in the few minutes between the visitor leaving and the arrival of Della Cookson. That's our assumption, is it?"

"It does look that way, sir."

"And do we know why Miss Cookson paid a visit so late at night?"

Hook shrugged his shoulders. "She's in the drawing room, sir. Waiting to be questioned. The housekeeper's with her."

Della was resplendent on an antique fainting couch. She looked like a poster for one of her plays. Flint, though briefly awestruck, managed to regain his habitual look of impassive appraisal.

"You were a patient of Dr. Rees, is that right?"

She gritted her teeth. "Yes, I'd been coming to see him for about a month."

"For what reason?"

"I don't see why I should answer that. It's got nothing to do with what happened here tonight, I can tell you that much."

Flint cocked his head amiably. "That's your prerogative. But please remember we'll have full access to the doctor's notes, so you may as well tell us."

But her lips were sealed.

Olive Turner sat by the window peering out, her face a ghoulish white. She jumped slightly when Flint approached her. "I'm sorry," she said, "I'm quite shaken."

"It's all right, perfectly understandable. I just wanted to ask you one or two questions while the events of tonight are still fresh in your mind."

The housekeeper flapped a hand vaguely. "Ask away."

"This visitor—the man who came to see Dr. Rees *before* Miss Cookson arrived. Are you completely sure this was someone you had never seen before?"

"Yes. He was a stranger. Everything about him. His face, his voice . . . it was almost as though he were in disguise. Like he was actively trying to conceal who he was."

"Why might that be, do you think?"

Olive turned her glassy eyes on him. "How should I know?"

"You said Dr. Rees was expecting him. Did the doctor give you any indication as to what the meeting was about?"

"None at all. But I assumed he must be a patient. The doctor kept his patient list very secret."

"And did he regularly see patients at night?"

"No. He kept strict office hours. That was why I was suspicious."

"And there was something about this man's behaviour that alarmed you?"

She thought for a moment. "He was a little like a wounded animal. There was something twitchy and off-kilter about him, like you never knew what he was going to do next. And he didn't know the house."

"What makes you say that?"

"When I told him the doctor was waiting in his study, he headed for the stairs. A return visitor would have known the study was on the ground floor. It stands to reason."

"Hm." Flint tapped his chin with a callused forefinger. "That's a very useful observation, thank you, Mrs. Turner."

Flint left the women and headed for the study again. His sergeant, Jerome Hook, accompanied him as he scribbled notes on a pad.

"All right," Flint began, "let's re-create the doctor's activities. He was working on his notes. Do we know what he was writing?"

"He was typing up an article for *The Alienist Review*. His notes are incomplete—in fact they cut off midsentence—as though he was interrupted."

"So it's safe to assume that he was working on this when Olive brought him his supper. And it was then that he gave her the strange instruction 'Do not show him in, simply direct him and let him find his own way to the office.' Why might he do a thing like that? I'm looking for suggestions."

Hook considered the question. "He didn't want Olive to overhear their conversation. *Any* of their conversation. Maybe she was an eavesdropper."

"Could be. We know she listened at the study door at least once. Right. So. She deposits the cheeseboard and leaves. Then, at quarter past eleven, she hears the visitor knocking at the door. We don't know what Dr. Rees was doing in the interim, but we can assume he was eating his supper and working on the article. So, the visitor arrives. Rees lets him into the study, locking them in. They conduct their business in secrecy and then the visitor leaves. His departure is witnessed by Olive. She goes to check on the doctor, but he does not let her into the study. We know he's alive, though, because he speaks to her through the door. What then? Olive makes her way up the stairs when she hears Della knocking at the front door—"

"No, that's wrong," Hook cut in. "You're forgetting the phone call."

"Why, so I am. The phone rings at eleven forty-five. Have we traced the call yet?"

"We have," said Hook, referring to his notepad. "Took me a little while, but I spoke to the girl at the exchange myself. The call was made from a flat in Dufresne Court. The place is registered to Floyd Stenhouse, the musician. He was one of the doctor's patients."

Flint grunted. He was tone-deaf and did not follow music. "Stenhouse. I'll speak to him presently. Right, what's next? Olive (God bless her inquisitive soul) listens to the conversation. Then she goes *back* to the kitchen to retrieve her book. And as she reenters the hallway, she sees Della Cookson on the doorstep. Therefore the murder must have occurred during the two minutes or so between the end of the telephone conversation and the arrival of Della Cookson. Does that seem fair?"

"It does, sir."

Flint smiled. "But at the same time, it's completely impossible."

As he spoke those words, Lidia Rees and Marcus Bowman arrived home. Hearing the commotion in the hallway, Flint went out to meet them. Marcus burbled and twitched with undue awkwardness in the presence of these stern-faced police types, but Lidia remained perfectly cool.

"Something's happened?" she said.

"I'm afraid so," said the inspector. "Are you Lidia Rees?"

"I am."

Flint gave a solemn nod. "Then I'm afraid I have some bad news for you. Is there somewhere we can talk?"

Lidia seemed untroubled as she led Flint up the stairs and into her bedroom. Flint stood beside her as she sat at the dressing table and began to remove her jewellery.

"Your father is dead, Miss Rees."

"I see."

"I'm sorry to say he was murdered. In his office."

"One of his patients?"

Flint was a little surprised by the question. "Were his patients violent?"

"Well, what else would it be? Robbery?"

"I suppose what I need to ask you, Miss Rees, is do you know why anybody would want to do any harm to your father?"

Lidia stared at herself in the mirror. For the first time, Flint noticed that her eyes brimmed with tears. "How did he die?" she said. Her voice was cool and crisp.

"His throat was cut."

"And do you have any suspects?"

"Not yet. That's why I need to ask you—can you think of any reason that somebody would want to hurt him?"

Slowly, she shook her head.

"Did you notice anything unusual in his behaviour? Did he seem worried or afraid at all?"

"My father was never afraid."

"Who was he expecting this evening?"

She considered the question. "Nobody. Not that I'm aware of, anyway."

"He had no appointments to your knowledge?"

"If he did, I would tell you."

Flint exhaled thoughtfully. "But he *did* have two visitors this evening."

Lidia turned away from her reflection to glare at the inspector. "Who?"

"A man in a trench coat. Mrs. Turner let him in."

"And who was it?"

"She doesn't know. It was a man she's never seen before. Can *you* think who it might have been?"

"If I could, I would tell you. Believe me."

"He spent some time with your father in the study. Mrs. Turner doesn't know what they talked about. Dr. Rees seemed eager to keep the circumstances of their meeting a secret."

Lidia hitched up her shoulders. "I see. No, my father mentioned nothing about this. Do you think this man was the murderer?"

"It would be the convenient assumption, but we have reason to believe your father was still alive when the man left. But naturally we'll need to speak to this fellow, whoever he is."

"And who was the second visitor?"

"Hm?"

"You mentioned my father had two visitors tonight."

"Ah. The second was his patient Della Cookson."

Lidia's jaw tightened. "Della. She's been coming to see him for several months."

"Well, she turned up very late, in some distress. She was desperate to see your father. She had something she needed to talk to him about. Do you have any idea what *that* might be? The lady is being somewhat evasive."

She shook her head. "I wish I did. Della is an interesting case."

"Did your father talk to you about his patients?"

"Of course. In a purely professional capacity."

"Why would she want to talk to him? Can you give me a general impression?"

There followed a long pause, during which Flint was able to take a sly sideways glance around the room. There were shelves lined with books and a large armoire, plus the luxuriant four-poster bed. But it was all somehow hollow and soulless, even after all these months of habitation.

"Do you think she killed my father?"

"We think the murder must have occurred at some point between the departure of the unidentified male visitor and Della's arrival."

"Then I can't tell you. My father would never countenance the breaking of a therapeutic confidence. Even if it would help to solve his murder."

"We'll be going through his notes, Lidia. We'll see all there is to see."

"I'm sure you will. But all the same, I value my integrity. My father would *never* permit me to devalue that by providing you with irrelevant information."

Flint nodded. "Fair enough. And to be perfectly frank, I'm more interested in the male visitor. Until we identify him, we won't have a chance of catching the killer. So if you think of anything—anything at all—to share with us, any nugget of information, no matter how small, then I would be very grateful."

He stood. "I'll leave you alone now, Miss Rees," he said. He made for the door. Then, almost as an afterthought, he turned back. "Oh, just one last thing. I don't suppose there's any kind of concealed entrance to your father's study?"

"What do you mean?"

"Apart from the hall door and the French windows, is there any other way a person could get into or out of the room?"

"No. Nothing like that."

Flint nodded. It was the answer he had been expecting. "Thank you, Miss."

And he left her alone.

On his way down the stairs, Inspector Flint heard Marcus Bowman firing questions at Sergeant Hook.

"What is it that's happened? What do you want? What have you done with Lidia? Where is she?"

"She's perfectly all right, Mr. Bowman," the Inspector supplied. "She's just had a shock, that's all."

Bowman headed for the stairs. "Then let me see her, I need to talk to her . . ."

Flint placed the palm of his hand in the centre of the young man's chest, holding him back. "Not just yet, sir. I need to ask you some questions."

"What is it? What's *happened*?"

"Dr. Anselm Rees is dead, sir. Murdered. He was killed within the last hour."

This silenced Marcus.

"I need to ask where you were this evening."

"I . . . I was with Lidia. All the time. She'll tell you. My God, you're not trying to tell me that you think I . . ."

"Where were you?"

"The Savoy. We, we had dinner there."

"And then?"

There followed an awkward silence. "A club. In Soho."

"Which one?"

"The Palmyra."

"And what time did you leave?"

"Just-just now. I mean, just a few minutes ago. We took a taxi here. I, I said I'd see her home."

"Very chivalrous of you, sir."

Bowman studied him blankly. "Well I . . . left my car here, you see."

Flint took Sergeant Hook to one side. "I want him questioned. I want the house searched. The slightest thing. A footprint. A fingerprint in the dust. Don't let anything slip past you. I'm going back to the station." He paused. "And then I shall need to visit someone."

"Yes sir. Who's that then, sir?"

A few hours later, around ten in the morning, London drowsed under a mire of drizzle as Inspector Flint emerged from the police car in Putney. The Black Pig public house loomed in front of him in its tumbledown splendour. After cleaning his mud-caked boots on the boot scraper, he headed inside.

The barmaid gestured wordlessly toward the snug. (Flint was a familiar face. She knew who he was after.) He headed through a low doorway into the next room, where threadbare armchairs were arranged artfully on the denuded floorboards before an unlit grate. A moth-eaten deer's head glowered down from the mantle.

Joseph Spector sat alone, riffling a deck of cards absently. Flint sat down opposite him.

"You're looking haggard," said the old magician without glancing up. "I don't believe you've shaved this morning."

"I've been working since midnight."

Spector's gaze snapped up. "Murder, is it? Anybody I would know?"

"A psychiatrist. Dr. Anselm Rees."

"*Rees* is dead? And who killed him?"

Flint steepled his fingers. It was what he did to show you he meant business. "Why do you think I'm sitting in front of you?"

"I *see* . . ." Spector leaned back, stretching his arms above his head. The gnarled knuckles crackled like twigs. He gave a yawn. "You'd better tell me everything."

Flint outlined the events of the previous evening in detail. He painted exacting pictures of the key players: Lidia Rees and Marcus Bowman, the housekeeper Olive Turner, and the actress Della Cookson.

When they'd first met a number of years before, Inspector Flint had viewed Spector with the guardedness he reserved for clever con men. After all, Spector was a famed devotee of the macabre and maintained one of the most comprehensive libraries on both crime and the supernatural. But it was this very "otherness" surrounding Spector that made him a perfect foil in instances of impossible crime. The useful part about knowing a magician is learning how the tricks are done.

He would never have called himself a recluse, but these days Spector tended to limit himself to a few local haunts. He'd lived at the curious, squat little house in Jubilee Court—a faintly Gothic-looking pile which, with lights blazing in its windows, seemed to resemble a hollowed-out skull—for as long as anyone could remember. But more often than not he was to be found here in the snug at the Black Pig, this ill-lit public house with its low beams, muntins on the windows, not to mention the brass taps and burbling old beer engine behind the bar. Some would call it dingy, but as any magician knows, the absence of light is a trickster's greatest ally.

"All right," said Joseph Spector. "So. The housekeeper, Olive Turner, do we trust her?"

"Yes. We do."

"Why?"

"Several reasons. One: she had nothing to gain from killing Doctor Rees. There was only a token provision for her in his will. Hardly worth killing over. Two: she'd only been working in the household for five months. I don't believe *that's* enough time to foster a lethal resentment. We've established pretty firmly that she and Dr. Rees had never met before Rees settled in England back in spring.

"And three," Flint continued, "for me this is the clincher: Della Cookson arrived at the house *after* the murder happened. And Olive let her in. If she'd just killed her employer, do you think she would have done something like that?"

"Fair enough. Your first two points are meaningless, but the third does carry some weight. Then what about this locked room? Give me the details."

"Two means of entry. The door, and the French windows. Both were locked on the inside."

"Is that it?"

"Yes. Trust me, we've been over that room again and again."

"No sign of a weapon?"

"None."

"And no way the doors could have been locked from the outside?"

"Not at all. In both cases, the key was in the lock."

"Any chance the glass in the windows might have been tinkered with?"

"None. As far as I'm concerned, Anselm Rees had his throat slit in a perfectly sealed room."

Joseph Spector gave a smile. "My favourite kind. Any other notable features of the room I ought to know about?"

"The usual. Desk. Bookshelves. Oh, and a trunk."

"What sort of trunk?"

"A big wooden one. But it was searched. It was completely empty."

"I see. I'll need to examine it for myself. But please go on."

"We found two sets of footprints in the rear garden of the house. But neither goes anywhere near the house itself, so we're hard-pressed to establish a link between the prints and the murder."

"Anything else?"

"We've been trying to get details out of Della Cookson, but she won't budge. Maybe you could have a try."

"Well, I can give you an alibi for her. She was at the producer Benjamin Teasel's house for most of the evening. Till around eleven o'clock. We all went there after the performance."

"Some kind of party, was it?"

"Yes. Teasel's a hound for that sort of affair. He loves the music, the dancing, the booze, the cigarette smoke."

"Not your scene, I wouldn't have thought?"

Spector smiled, split the deck of cards in two, and then slid them together again. Flint had no way of knowing it, but the old man had just performed a perfect weave shuffle, flawlessly interlacing the two halves of the deck. "You'll be surprised what an old man will put up with for the sake of an attentive audience."

"And how long was she at the party?"

"I can't be entirely sure, but I know that she was there at ten thirty, and that she was gone by eleven."

"She left by cab?"

"I believe so. Teasel's house, I should point out, is in Hampstead."

Flint nodded. "So it would have taken at least twenty minutes to reach the house in Dollis Hill. And she arrived just after the telephone call."

"Telephone call," Spector repeated, "yes, we'll get to that. For now I'm more interested in Della Cookson. Was she searched?"

"We looked in her handbag. Needless to say, she was reluctant. But there was nothing of interest. Why? You don't think *she* could have done it, do you? I mean, there's no way she could have got into the study to kill the doctor. And even if she did, why would she *then* go around to the front door—?"

"Let me stop you there," Spector interrupted. "While I admit that it's unlikely she could have killed Rees in the circumstances you describe, I think we ought to be careful before we underestimate her part in the case."

Flint opened his mouth, but he didn't speak.

"What I mean is this," Spector went on. "Do you have any way of knowing the *real* reason for her visit last night?"

Now Flint shook his head slowly.

"Or any idea why she became one of the doctor's patients in the first place? The night before last was opening night for her new play, *Miss Death*. It's at the Pomegranate, and I happen to have worked on the production. It looks set to be a hit. So last night, after the second night of the run, the producer held a party at his town house. The cast was there, the playwright, the director, and various high-profile figures from that circle.

"Now, my point is this: something happened at that party, Inspector Flint, which may cast the murder in a new light."

"Are you going to tell me or not?"

Spector grinned. "Benjamin Teasel is a producer. He lives or dies depending on whether or not a show will run. And I happen to know that this morning Teasel was talking about cancelling tonight's performance. So hopefully that gives you an inkling as to how serious this is."

"More serious than murder?"

"To Benjamin, yes. During the party at his town house, he was burgled."

"And what does that have to do with Della Cookson?"

"So you haven't read the doctor's notes yet?"

Flint shook his head.

"She's a kleptomaniac. A compulsive thief. It's an open secret at the Pomegranate, and the problem has become so severe that she sought the help of Dr. Rees. This is entirely off the record, you understand," he added parenthetically, "but last night—before she visited the doctor—Della stole something of almost unappreciable value."

"Tell me," said Flint.

So Spector did. He began to recount everything he had seen for himself, alongside the accounts of others present.

The party at Benjamin Teasel's house was almost putrid in its decadence. The centrepiece was a pyramid of champagne glasses, and a jazz trio honked away at the far end of the room while the young crew and company of *Miss Death* swung each other round and round in a whirligig of limbs.

Teasel himself adored playing host and had dressed for the occasion in a bright red smoking jacket, so there was no risk of his being lost in the crowd. Typically, he would stand proprietorially over the most important members of the company, snaring them in a conversational web from which they could not quite extricate themselves. Naturally, his focus was on Della Cookson.

Spector, meanwhile, established himself in the far corner of the ballroom, smoking his cigarillos and unburdening Teasel of several glasses of liqueur. Though Spector prided himself on his almost uncanny observational skills, he had to admit that the night of the party was not his finest hour. He concentrated a little too much on amusing his companions with a few old card and coin tricks to fully pay attention to Teasel and Della when they drifted toward him.

At some point, Spector was certain, Benjamin Teasel and Della Cookson left the party and went upstairs. They were gone about ten minutes. And then, when they returned, Della said a few hasty goodbyes and left the party altogether. That was eleven o'clock, or thereabouts. Teasel seemed a little non-plussed by his leading lady's sudden flight. But not quite so nonplussed as he was an hour later, at the stroke of midnight, when the theft was discovered.

He strode to the front of the room and silenced the jazz trio with an abrupt wave. "Ladies and gentlemen!" he roared above the murmurs rippling through the crowd. "Nobody is to leave. There has been a robbery."

"So what did she take?" Flint wanted to know.

"Only one item. It was a painting: *El Nacimiento* by the 'mad Spaniard' Manolito Espina."

"And what makes you so sure Della was the one who took it?"

"It's the only assumption. She was the only one who left the party, and therefore the only one who wasn't searched."

"Couldn't a burglar have got into the house from the outside?"

"All the windows and doors were locked up tight. Except, that is, for the front door. But Teasel had two maids stationed there to admit latecomers. And they say there were no intruders."

"Well. That is very strange indeed."

"In fact, I just got off the telephone with Benjamin Teasel before you arrived here this morning. He's most keen to get his property back."

"What did he say to you?"

"He wants me to look into the case."

Flint sat back in his chair, incredulous. "Why?"

Spector shrugged. "He trusts me. He knows I have a certain knack for these things."

"Did he tell you anything else?"

"He did. He gave me his version of last night's events."

—⁎—

"Come with me. I want to show you something."

With a tipsy Della Cookson on his arm, Benjamin Teasel headed out of the ballroom where the festivities were in full swing. He led her up a spiral staircase to a small side room. On a cord around his neck hung a pair of keys, one large and one small. With the large key he unlocked the door.

"Why have you brought me up here, Benny?" said Della, whispering playfully in the darkness.

"I'm showing you something. Something which I *know* you're going to appreciate. You are a person of culture and sensibility, after all."

Moonlight streamed through the single window into the sparsely furnished spare bedroom. With a painful grunt, Teasel knelt down beside the narrow single bed and pulled out from under it a large wooden chest. Using the small key around his neck, he unlocked the chest and lifted the lid. "Please," he said, gesturing for Della to approach.

And there, with the throb and blast of the jazz and dancing beneath them, she took her first and last look at Benjamin Teasel's treasure. Facing them from within the velvet-lined chest was an oblong painting in a giltwood frame.

"My God," said Della.

"I know," answered Teasel, aglow with pride. "Isn't she beautiful?"

To try and describe such a work is inevitably a vain task. The art lies somewhere between subject and canvas. But the painting depicted a young woman, cradling in her arms an infant. The woman's face was smooth as porcelain, the skin infused with the pinkish glow of joy and beatific innocence. The child, eyes screwed shut and mouth midshriek, was perfectly rendered. You could almost hear the cry.

"*El Nacimiento*, by Manolito Espina," Teasel announced. "Isn't she divine?"

Della stared down at the painting.

"You'll forgive an old fool his grandiosity, but I couldn't resist the chance to share this with someone who would truly appreciate it."

"Where did you get it?" asked Della.

"On my travels," came the answer, "from a person who had little inkling as to the work's true value. Well, Della? What do you have to say?"

"It's . . . dazzling," she told him, not taking her eyes off the canvas. "What are you going to do with it?"

"Do? Della, it's mine. I don't have to do anything with it."

"You're not going to share it or display it or anything like that?"

"I would never put something like this on show, it would be too vulgar. It would detract from what is essentially a religious experience. And as for sharing . . . well, I'm sharing it with you now."

"And you're going to keep it here, under the bed?"

"You may not know it, Della darling," Teasel began, "but this painting is alive. It breathes. That's why I keep it in this room, in this chest. This is the only room in the house with adequate air. The painting is a curmudgeonly old thing and doesn't care for sunlight or fluctuations in temperature. They would cause it to crack and curl. But by moonlight, it looks simply sublime."

Della had to agree. In its giltwood frame of murky gold there could be no room for doubt: this was the real thing.

The corners of Teasel's mouth creased, as though with satisfaction. He had achieved his desired effect. "Give me your honest verdict."

"I . . ." began Della. Then she stumbled sideways, brushing Teasel with her elbow. He slammed shut the chest, jamming the key into the keyhole. And with a quick twist of his wrist,

El Nacimiento was secure. He then replaced the pair of keys around his neck, and turned his attentions to the leading lady.

"My dear! What's the matter?"

"Nothing," she said softly, "nothing at all." Her gaze was fixed on the chest.

Teasel led her down the staircase and back to the festivities. But not before locking the bedroom door behind him.

"I think I'm going to call it a night," said Della over the blare of the band.

"If that's what you want, sweetheart," said Teasel. She snaked her arms around this rotund little figure and gave him a peck on the cheek.

Joseph Spector caught up with her on her way to the door. "Something the matter, Della?"

"I have to see someone," she said.

"Everything all right?"

But she was gone. The door swung shut behind her. It was not yet raining and the streets were deathly quiet. Spector heard her heels echoing on stone as she strode away.

Manolito Espina—who died around 1820—was as much famed for his ignominious descent into insanity in the final decade of his life as for the canvases that would survive him. His most celebrated work, *The Yard at the End of the World*, currently resides in the National Gallery. Even now it causes outrage among the more conservative sections of society.

That a piece of that nature could be placed in such auspicious surroundings!

The epithet he acquired in his lifetime, and which still taints his legacy, is "El Desquiciato"—The Deranged. People tend to forget that Espina was not merely a schizophrenic, and the image of him as a frothing lunatic has been hard to dispel. But *El Nacimiento* was the product of his happier, youthful days. Before the darkness fell across his life. The features of the subject are so soft and delicate in texture that one might almost reach out and touch them.

The idea most people have of Manolito Espina is of the crazed hermit he eventually became, slathering canvases in darkness and depravity. But Teasel's acquisition was the work of a younger, more sensitive artist. The caterwauling baby in its mother's arms, that real sense of maternal affection in the young woman's eyes which somehow transcended the mere material and paint. These days people associate Espina with tattered, ruined flesh and biblical tortures. The horrors of the Inquisition, or else a whirl of dark, wicked spirits. But to do so is to neglect his knack for capturing more benign human frailties. Emotion and affection. Raw love, like a heart laid bare. The subjects of *El Nacimiento* were anonymous, which only added to their ethereal wonder, and made one question whether the mad Spaniard was really so mad after all.

The only established facts were that Teasel had possessed the painting up until last night, and now he did not. It was locked away in a box, in a darkened room. There was only one key to the room and to the box, both of which were kept on a chain around Teasel's neck. They had gleamed beneath the chandeliers as he danced with his guests. And then, like a magic trick, both keys and the painting were gone.

The party skidded to a halt. The police were called. Everybody—every single guest—was accounted for and searched by police. This caused considerable indignation. Even Spector had to endure the indignity. But the painting was gone. And the only guest unaccounted for was Della Cookson.

When Spector had finished describing all these events to the inspector, Flint sat for a moment, thoughtfully considering the deer's head above the mantle.

"What about the frame?" Flint asked.

"Oh, the whole thing's gone all right. Not a trace of painting *or* frame," Spector said almost gleefully. "The window was bolted on the inside, but of course it was much too small to remove the painting anyway. All in all, and factoring in the giltwood frame, *El Nacimiento* was two feet in height and one foot in width. And yet the square window in the bedroom was scarcely eight inches. So what does that leave us? It leaves us with the fact that the painting *must* have been brought down one or other of the staircases. If it had been brought down the servants' staircase, it would have had to be carried through the ballroom to the front door. I find it hard to believe even the most ardent reveller could have missed it. That leaves us with the main staircase, out in the hall. But there was always at least one maid at the foot of that staircase the whole time. And of course, the spectacle of a guest carrying a large and priceless painting would no doubt have attracted their attention. Resulting in rather a prickly problem, I think you'll agree."

"I'll need to interview Teasel," said Flint.

"I'd advise against that."

"Why?"

"Because he'll clam up. Remember, he may have come by the painting through somewhat unscrupulous means. He didn't even want people to know he *had* the painting. So if an inspector turns up on his doorstep bleating about murder, I can guarantee that he'll run screaming for the nearest lawyer."

Flint grunted. "Maybe you're right. From what you're saying, it sounds as though he hadn't managed to get it insured. But what's all this got to do with Rees's death?"

"I don't know. Possibly nothing. But what's undeniable is that Della Cookson was at the scene of not one but *two* major crimes last night. An art theft and an impossible murder. So I'm sure she'll have plenty to tell us."

Spector produced from behind his ear a cigarillo, which he slipped between his narrow lips and lit with a match. "But I think we had better bide our time. I know Della—she's rather like a deer or some such woodland creature. If we get too close, come on too strong, she'll bolt."

"Prickly, aren't you, you theatre types?" Flint offered with a wry lip-twitch.

"Well," said Spector, "we'd better get going, hadn't we?"

"Where to?"

Spector picked up his deck of cards and, with a flutter of his fingers, they disappeared. "Why, Dollis Hill, of course," he said.

VI

DER SCHLANGENMANN

The Rees house swarmed with uniformed officers. The corpse was gone, but the carpet in the late doctor's office was now crisp with dried blood, and the air hung with a coppery odour. Flint and Spector—who was kitted out with his cloak and silver cane—studied the room by daylight. But of course, there was only one conclusion to be reached. The door was locked when the doctor died. So were the windows. And once locked, they were impermeable. Spector even studied the empty wooden trunk. But there was nothing to see.

"Where's the doctor's daughter?" he asked.

"In the lounge."

"May I speak with her?"

"By all means."

Flint led the way out of the study and into the adjacent lounge. Lidia Rees was subdued and statuesque, silhouetted in the rain-spattered bay window.

"And who is this?" she said.

"I'm Joseph Spector," the old man answered. "I'm very sorry for your loss."

"Thank you for your concern. I've seen you before, haven't I? At the theatre two nights ago?"

Distinctly dry-eyed and almost clinical in her dissection of the evening's events, she answered Spector's questions openly.

"If I understand the situation correctly," Lidia said, her voice threaded with ice, "then my father was killed under circumstances which couldn't possibly be. A victim of something very sinister indeed. Killed by a ghost, you might say."

"Well," answered Spector, his voice crisp and urbane, "that's what we are here to determine."

"Marcus and I were together all evening. We went out to dinner, and then drinks at the Palmyra."

"I see. So. Dinner. Where was this?"

"The Savoy. We arrived at eight—the reservation will be on their books and I don't believe you'll find a shortage of witnesses. We were there till around ten; the maître d'hôtel will be able to give you a more concrete idea of time. From the Savoy, we hopped straight into a cab. I don't have the number, I'm afraid, but perhaps the doormen will be able to advise."

"And from there—straight to the Palmyra?"

"Correct. A ten-minute journey, and the doormen at the Palmyra can no doubt attest to our arrival."

"How long were you there?"

"Until midnight at least. I'm afraid I can't be sure. But Marcus will provide my alibi, as I will provide his. We came back to the house together. The rest you know."

"I see. What can you tell us about your father's patients?"

"There were three—only three. My father frequently discusses—" she corrected herself "—*discussed* their cases with me. I also had access to his notes. This was purely a professional concern, you understand. I knew none of them personally."

"But you *met* them, surely?"

"I was never present during consultations."

"So—who was the first?"

"Patient A (as my father refers to him in the notes) is Floyd Stenhouse, the concert musician. He was the first to seek out my father when we arrived in this country. Patient B is Della Cookson, whom you know. Patient C is the novelist Claude Weaver. He was referred to us by his wife, who was concerned for his mental state."

"And can you give me any details on the treatments your father offered?"

"My father kept fastidious notes. It's all there. There is not much beyond that which I can tell you."

"Nothing personal, no minor observations?"

"Forgive me," Lidia said. "My mind is not working properly."

"Nothing at all? No enmity or aggravation or capacity for violence?"

She fixed Spector with a steady gaze. "Look to the notes. If the answer is anywhere, it will be there."

"You'll forgive me for saying this," Spector persisted, "but you're very calm and collected under the circumstances."

She studied him, unblinking. "The sad truth of the matter is that my father died a long time ago. The part of him that can think and feel dropped down dead many years before we even left Vienna. His bodily death was just the inevitable aftermath."

"What do you mean by that?"

She sighed and steeled herself to broach what was evidently a troubling subject. "The papers in Vienna called him *Der Schlangenmann*. 'The Snakeman.'"

"Who?"

"He was one of my father's patients. A very troubling case. This was many years ago, of course. I was only ten."

"I'm sorry," Flint cut in, "but is this relevant to your father's murder?"

"I'm certain of it. The Snakeman was obsessed by a recurring dream in which he was terrorised by an immense snake. My father diagnosed him—correctly—as suffering from filial paranoia. The snake was his child, a daughter. And the dream indicated an unhealthy, insidious bond between the two. All of this is a matter of public record—my father published extensive notes on the case."

"And you think the Snakeman was the cause of last night's murder?"

Lidia blinked at him and chewed her lip. "For several months the Snakeman was a live-in patient at my father's clinic just outside Vienna. The treatment was intensive. But it failed. It was my father's only failure."

"So . . . he couldn't cure the Snakeman?"

"One morning my father paid a visit to the Snakeman in his quarters and found him in bed with his throat slit. A razor blade hung limply from his right hand. The horror of this incident stayed with my father for the rest of his life. It was not so much the death of the Snakeman as it was the sense of having failed in his diagnosis. A better clinician, he sometimes said, would have been able to prevent the man's death. He could not bear that he was unable to see the treatment through to its conclusion."

"And what can you tell me about the Snakeman himself?"

"The treatment took place over eleven weeks in the autumn of 1921 at his clinic in the Wachau Valley, but the case study was not published until 1925. And then only grudgingly. Like all of my father's writings, it caused a sensation. But the question of the Snakeman's identity was never answered."

"Do *you* know who it was?" Spector asked.

Lidia shook her head. "It's a secret my father kept all his life. I only found out the circumstances of the Snakeman's death a few years ago, when I was commencing my own doctoral studies. I think my father considered it a rite of passage for me. A dire warning too."

"What sort of warning?"

"About the dangers of playing God. Of trying to force your will onto another. A warning about the nature of a psychiatrist's power."

"But why do you think your father's death has anything to do with this Snakeman?"

"As far as I can tell, I am the only living person to whom my father confided the circumstances of the poor fellow's death. Apart from the authorities, of course. And for those circumstances to repeat themselves here . . ."

"It's too much of a coincidence," Spector supplied.

"As I said, it's all a matter of public record. I have a copy of the notes somewhere." She skimmed the shelves and eventually retrieved a leather-bound volume. She handed it to Spector, who flipped it open and studied the title page: *The Case Studies of Anselm Rees.*

"May I borrow this?"

"Of course. Maybe when you've read it you'll see why I can't escape the idea that my father's death might in fact be a *suicide.*"

Flint and Spector looked at each other. Then Flint said carefully: "I have to tell you, suicide does seem particularly unlikely. To begin with, no weapon was found in the study. Nothing at all which your father could have used to inflict that wound on himself. And of course, it doesn't help us identify the man who visited him that night."

A faint smile flickered round the corners of Lidia's lips. "I think perhaps you've underestimated quite how clever my father was."

"Oh really?"

"Well . . . did you consider the possibility that the visitor may have been . . . my father himself?"

Flint snorted involuntarily. "What gives you that idea, Miss?"

"His reasons may be tricky to discern. But I think my father used poor Olive as an unwilling stooge for some sort of devilment."

"But why should he do that?" Spector demanded. "Why convince her that he received a visitor when in fact the visitor was himself?"

"There's a profound sense of shame which he attached to the notion of suicide. The indignity of it. It would be difficult for a man like my father to countenance. Perhaps he was orchestrating a vanishing murderer so that the truth of his sad death would not be public knowledge."

"Was he capable of something like that?"

She sighed. "This is a problem of psychology as much as pathology. What you have to consider is that my father was a virtuoso of the mind. And that every thought coursing through your head as we speak now has probably already been considered by him. You are following the exact path that he laid out for you."

Flint sat back in his seat. "A sort of double-double bluff, you mean? He created an impossible crime to conceal the fact it was no crime at all?"

She shrugged. "You're the detective. All I can tell you is that my father is dead. But the case of the Snakeman has a certain bilateral symmetry with the present circumstances, don't you think? Der Schlangenmann cut his throat, Inspector. A single gash crossways with a razor blade, but the violence, the sheer *savagery* of that stroke was enough to almost decapitate him. Can you imagine the torment that would induce someone to commit such an abomination upon themselves?"

"No," said Flint with strident solemnity. "I'm afraid I can't."

"My father could," Lidia added. "Perhaps you should think about that."

They left Lidia alone soon after. Clearly she had nothing more to tell them.

"I want to see the housekeeper," Spector said to Flint in hushed tones as they departed from the study.

They found her in the kitchen. She was doing her level best to pretend the previous night's events were merely a nightmare. She bustled about, dusting things and boiling kettles, and generally doing a decent job of looking busy.

Olive Turner had a face that might be called gentle, with dark, deep-set eyes and a faintly curled upper lip, giving her an aspect of almost biblical serenity. She was in her early fifties, a childless widow, and wore bulky dresses and woollen cardigans, with her hair in tight-set curls. There was in her appearance and her bearing a modesty that was belied by her strident East London accent, known affectionately among her friends as her "fish-hawker's squawk."

When he had finally convinced her to sit down at the kitchen table, Spector began his questioning gently. "Do you like your mistress?"

"Miss Rees? Certainly, she's a sweet and clever young lady."

"She tells us she went out last night with her young man, is that right?"

"Yes. He called earlier in the day."

"On the telephone?"

"Yes."

"And did you speak to him?"

"I did. Miss Rees didn't want to talk to him, so I took the message."

Spector frowned. "Didn't you think that was rather strange?"

"Well yes, now you mention it. But then, she is a funny girl. Hard to work out, you know what I mean?"

"Did she seem angry at all?"

"A little. But then, she always seems fairly irate. It's just her nature. You know these European types, God love 'em."

"But she gave no indication of it when he arrived to pick her up?"

"I wasn't around to see, sir. I was in the kitchen doing the doctor's dinner."

"What did he have?"

"Beef, sir. And potatoes."

"Ate it up, did he?"

"Yes, sir. And the cheese I brought him for afters."

"Now, Mrs. Turner, I'm going to ask you a question—and I don't want to alarm you. But I need you to be honest and answer in as much detail as you can."

Mrs. Turner swallowed. "Whatever I can do to help."

"I need you to tell me about the man who visited the house last night."

Mrs. Turner's eyes darkened like rolling thunderheads. "All I can tell you, sir, is that I hope I never lay eyes on him again as long as I live."

VII

DUFRESNE COURT

Spector and Flint made a hasty departure from Dollis Hill. Spector claimed to have seen all he needed to see. But at the same time, he looked strangely dissatisfied.

"Well, where do we go from here?" said Flint once they were back in the car.

Spector considered the question. "You mentioned something about a telephone call?"

"You mean Floyd Stenhouse? Patient A? He called the house and spoke to Dr. Rees on the telephone just a minute or two before the murder."

Spector nodded. "Good. We'll visit him next." And they sped away.

Floyd Stenhouse lived (when he was not touring the world with the illustrious Philharmonic) in an elegant art deco flat in Dufresne Court, near Cranley Gardens. The frontage of the building resembled nothing so much as bleak, faceless slate, like some dystopian vision from a film by Murnau.

Dufresne Court was a block of sixty flats, piled up in six storeys. Its curved façade looked out on Quarterhouse Square, and it was designed in the new art deco style, built from beige brick and patterned with brutalist mullions. A luxury residence, where a man might lose himself, or hide himself away from the world. Stenhouse's address was on the fourth floor—Spector stood on the pavement outside, looking up and trying to pinpoint the window. A futile task, for it turned out that Stenhouse's apartment overlooked the cobbled courtyard to the rear of the building, and was not visible from the street.

Spector and Flint headed into the marbled foyer. Flint strode purposefully toward the front desk, where a porter surveyed the two men from behind his logbook. "Can I help you gentlemen?" he said.

"You can," said Flint, slapping his warrant card down on the table. "We're here to see Floyd Stenhouse."

"Is he expecting you, sir?" The fellow was unruffled.

Flint leaned forward, his elbows creasing the leaves of the logbook. "Don't be silly now. Where is he?"

"Four-oh-eight. Fourth floor."

Spector also leaned in close. "And what is your name, sir?"

The desk clerk gave an almost comical double take, as though this were the first time he had ever been asked such a question. "Royce," he said. "Royce is my name."

Spector clicked his fingers and from the empty air plucked a business card. "A number, Royce. Between one and ten. Quickly now, there's a good fellow."

Flummoxed, the man said: "Seven."

"Ah," Spector was pleased. "I thought so." He turned the card over in his fingers, revealing the number seven handwritten on its underside. He handed it over. "Keep that, Royce, as a souvenir of this day." And he breezed away.

"What was that about?" said Flint as they strode toward the elevator.

"Elementary, if you'll forgive the flagrant appropriation. A smidge of graphite under the thumbnail."

"No. I mean, why do you want to know about the desk clerk?"

"Superciliousness. It's a disease rife among the desk clerks of high-class apartment buildings. I find it helps to catch them off guard once in a while."

Flint had begun to notice something interesting about Joseph Spector. The "old man" seemed to grow older or younger depending on who it was he was talking to. Depending on which offered the greater advantage. It was a subtle, almost imperceptible transformation, but damned effective. His shoulders would ease back, his spine would straighten. He might grow up to three inches or so in height. But more troublingly still, his *face* would become younger. The creases would fade, and those pale eyes would deepen. That silver-topped cane of his would become a mere stylistic accessory.

Or else he would shrink and shrivel, his physical frailty would become more pronounced. His voice might even develop an uncomfortable quivery undertone. Truly remarkable. He could age decades before your very eyes. In many ways it was the most fascinating trick Flint had ever seen him perform.

The boy who operated the elevator looked like a refugee from one of the more esteemed American hotels. He wore red uniform lined in gold trim, and a little pillbox hat affixed to his head by a chinstrap. He was perhaps sixteen years old and bounced jovially on the balls of his feet as he admitted the two gents to his domain.

"Got friends here, have you?" he inquired chirpily as they headed up.

Flint eyed the boy, his jaw clenched. Spector, however, was more forthcoming. "We're here to visit a gentleman who lives on the fourth floor. Mr Stenhouse."

"Aah," said the boy. "Well, that explains it."

"Explains what?" Flint asked sharply.

"Come to take him away, have you? I always said he was doolally."

"Now why do you say that?"

"He's a . . . whatdoyoucallit? A recluse. Scared of the world and everything in it. How someone like that can survive in London I'll never know."

"What's your name, young man?"

"Pete Hobbs, sir."

"And how long have you worked here?"

"About a year, sir."

"Anything *specific* you can tell us about his behaviour?"

Pete Hobbs narrowed his eyes and peered at the middle distance in a pantomime of acute consideration. "Very set in his ways. Like for instance, we had the chaps in to repair the elevator last week. Blimey, you'd have thought it was the end of the world. Mr. Stenhouse had a good rave down at the front desk, bellowing about the inconvenience."

"Anything else?"

"Stingy—not a tipper. Plays his bloody violin at all hours too, if you'll pardon the French."

Flint and Spector exchanged a humourous glance. "And that's it?" said Flint.

"All due respect, sir, I think that's quite enough."

With a clatter, the elevator reached its destination. Pete wrenched open the cage and stood expectantly as his passengers filed out. Almost as an afterthought, Spector handed him half a crown. "Most kind of you, sir," said the boy. "God bless."

"Well, what do you think?" Spector asked Flint in a low voice as the two men strode side by side along the corridor.

"I think this Stenhouse sounds like a prime candidate for Rees's treatment."

They rapped on the door of flat 408. "Who's that?" came the answer from inside.

"Inspector Flint, sir. Scotland Yard."

And the door was opened a crack. The man who greeted them, Patient A, was not what Spector had anticipated all. For one thing, he was tall. All this talk of emotional frailty had given Spector the mental image of an almost gnomish figure scuttling between shadows. But this fellow was over six feet in height, slightly paunched, though the limbs were narrow and angular, like the décor of the building.

His face, round as a dinner plate, was quite handsome in an unimaginative kind of way. It was what a small child might have drawn if tasked with drawing a hero or a film star. But it lacked definition or expression, and the close-set dark eyes blinked a little too often.

"Police? What do you want?"

"I believe you were a patient of Dr. Anselm Rees?"

Stenhouse took a sharp intake of breath. "Were . . ." he repeated.

"Yes, I'm afraid something has happened to Dr. Rees. In fact, he's been murdered."

Whatever reaction Spector had anticipated, this was not it. Stenhouse simply stood back to let them into his flat.

"I'm sorry to break the news to you like this, sir," Flint went on. "It happened last night."

"Murdered," Stenhouse repeated, enunciating the word with almost palpable relish.

"And so naturally we need to interview all the late doctor's patients. To get an idea as to who might have wanted to do such a thing to him."

And then the dam burst: Stenhouse let fly a torrent of untrammelled verbosity. "Gentlemen, you must forgive me, I'm unused to receiving visitors at this hour and the news you bring is not only shocking but also deeply troubling to me at a very personal level, this is an appalling crime, the very worst, and I want you to know that I will do whatever I can to help you catch the devil, anything at all, you just have to ask; you see, Dr. Rees was a hero to me, an idol, the only man I would trust with my dreams and my secrets and the horrors of my wretched brain—"

Flint cut him short. "It happened last night, around midnight. Where were you at that time?"

Stenhouse froze. "Around midnight," he repeated. It was an alarming tic, this repetition. "I was here at midnight. In bed."

"Have you anybody to corroborate that?"

Stenhouse's eyelid twitched. "What do you mean by that? I'm telling you the truth. I was here in bed. In fact, I . . ." Now he trailed off.

"Yes?" Spector prompted.

"Just before twelve I . . . made a telephone call."

"What can you tell us about the call?"

"For a long time I've been suffering with nightmares. But not just ordinary nightmares. I dread the twilight hours. Dr. Rees has been helping me to make sense of them. And of my own brain. And last night I went to bed at about eleven. I had a particularly troubling dream, from which I awoke at about half past eleven. I was so distressed by it that I immediately telephoned the doctor himself. It was impetuous of me, I admit. But I needed to speak to someone."

"So you spoke to the doctor at half past eleven. How did he seem?"

"Perfectly normal. A little perturbed that I had telephoned him so late, which I admit is understandable."

"So, to confirm," said the Inspector, "you have no way of *proving* that you were here alone all evening?"

Stenhouse was affronted. "You can ask the elevator boy, Peter. He'll tell you I didn't go out at all."

"Well, he'll tell us that you didn't take the *elevator*. But surely a great modern edifice like this one possesses both an elevator and a staircase?"

Stenhouse spoke through gritted teeth: "Then speak to the doormen. Or the night attendant. They'll tell you I did not go out. That I was *here* all night. And besides, you must have record of the telephone call?"

Flint nodded. "Please don't misunderstand," he said, suddenly conciliatory, "we just need to establish all the facts. I don't mean to cause offence."

"Well you should be careful about how you speak to people. Of all the people in the world, I would *never* do anything to hurt Dr. Rees. Truly, he was the only one who could have helped me. He was such a noble man, as all Viennese are. I went there once with the Philharmonic. A wonderful city."

"Your telephone conversation," interjected Spector, attempting to bring the conversation back on track. "Can you tell us anything specific the doctor said to you? Anything out of the ordinary or unusual in some way?"

Stenhouse ruminated. "He chided me for calling so late. But he also agreed that the dream itself was interesting. He made a note of it for us to discuss later. And he invited me to visit him tomorrow—that is, today."

"And what was the dream?"

"What has that to do with anything?"

Spector gave an embarrassed little smile. "Just idle curiosity. I'm sure it has no relevance."

"The dream is between myself and Dr. Rees. I don't wish to discuss it with you. And you can't compel me to without a warrant."

"Even with a warrant," Flint supplied, "I think we'd struggle."

"Very well then. Now please, leave me in peace. I'm not a well man."

"Have you had decorators recently, Mr. Stenhouse?" Spector inquired, looking around the apartment. His gaze was caught by a small, round-faced alarm clock by the window. A curious place for it, he thought; was Stenhouse prone to falling asleep at the window?

"Decorators? Why?"

"I thought I could smell paint."

"An olfactory hallucination," said Stenhouse. "A psychiatrist could help you with that."

Flint and Spector left the apartment soon after, just as Stenhouse was helping himself to a scotch from a tray on a nearby cabinet. Stenhouse downed it in one, and when he replaced the glass, it did not clatter but landed silently on the softness of the rubber-topped surface.

On their way out of Dufresne Court, Flint took a detour to the front desk. "Were you on duty last night?" he asked the porter.

"I was, sir," answered Royce.

"And did you see Floyd Stenhouse at all during the evening?"

"Mr Stenhouse? Can't say I did."

"He didn't come down to the lobby at all?"

"Not that I saw. As I recall, he'd been performing at a concert that night. He came home at about ten o'clock."

"He went straight up to the apartment?"

"Yes, sir."

"And he didn't come down again?"

"No, sir."

"Is there any other way he could have got out of the building unobserved?"

"I should say not. That would take him either through the kitchens or the laundry room. Anyone would have seen him. I happen to know there were staff at work in those two rooms throughout the night."

Flint nodded, satisfied. They left the building.

"So what have we got?" demanded the inspector.

"Several disparate threads. Benjamin Teasel's painting for one, apparently stolen by Della Cookson—though we've no idea how she got it out from under everyone's noses."

"Mm. And what about all this Snakeman nonsense?"

"Hard to say. The similarities between the two deaths is hard to ignore, even if they're separated by countries and decades. But until we find out more about the Snakeman case it's going to be difficult to determine. For instance, have you considered that this Snakeman may have left a family behind, who might have blamed Rees for the poor fellow's suicide?"

"And what about what Lidia said? Do you think her father was clever or crazy enough to pull off a suicide scheme like that?"

"Honestly, no. But I've been wrong before." Spector strode on.

"Then what's next?" Flint eventually asked. "Della Cookson?"

"Not yet. We have met Patient A. We've both had our encounters with Patient B. It's time we met Patient C, don't you think?"

VIII

PATIENT C

"The sad truth of it is," Rosemary Weaver began, "my husband just hasn't been himself lately."

They sat in her parlour with its olive green décor and its damp, musty ambiance, and Joseph Spector reflected that he had scarcely encountered an uglier room. The Weavers lived in Hampstead, by chance only a couple of streets away from Benjamin Teasel.

Rosemary Weaver, smiling, poured the tea. After a murky start, the day had turned out bright and crisp. Last night's rainfall had left a cool freshness in the air.

"In what way 'not himself?'" asked Spector.

"Quiet. Subdued. And lately he confessed to me a certain strange fear."

"And what might that be?"

She leaned forward. Her voice was a whisper: "That he may be losing his mind."

A glance passed between Spector and Flint.

"I can *assure* you," Rosemary persisted, "that I never believed it myself. Claude has always been a worrier. And he's had so much on his mind lately."

"And so he began consulting Dr. Rees?"

"It was my suggestion. I handle the majority of my husband's business affairs. I arranged that initial meeting. And I keep a close monitor on his progress."

"Did your husband ever demonstrate what you might think of as violent tendencies?"

Mrs Weaver outright guffawed. "Gentlemen! My husband is the most benevolent soul you'll ever meet. Don't let those novels of his mislead you. He's very good at conjuring up an air of dread and suspense, but in his real life he is a perfectly well-behaved English gentleman. Rather shy and unassuming. He *loathes* being the centre of attention."

"And where is he now, if I may ask?"

"In the garden. But he'll be back momentarily."

"I see. In the meantime, I just have one more question."

"By all means."

"Do you know where your husband was last night?"

The smile on her face stretched until it became a masklike rictus. "A meeting with his publisher. But surely you don't mean that you suspect my husband may be involved with the doctor's death?" Off Flint's look, she explained: "My husband and I saw it in this morning's papers."

"We're obliged to pursue all avenues of inquiry, madam," said Flint with practiced pomposity. "Now who is this publisher?"

"Tweedy is his name. Never cared for him myself. Rather vulgar, as these new-money types tend to be."

At that point—to everyone's relief—Claude Weaver entered the room. Unlike Floyd Stenhouse, his was a cooler and more composed presence. He was in his shirtsleeves, with a cigarette hanging limply from his lips. He was balding and bony, but his face had a certain ruddy attractiveness. He did not seem startled by the presence of these two strangers.

"Oh," he said.

Introductions were made, and the writer was quickly apprised of the situation. He sat beside his wife, nodding slowly and tapping his cigarette ash into a spare teacup.

"Your wife tells us you were at a meeting with your publisher last night," Flint prompted.

"That's right. Tweedy."

"I see," Flint said, scribbling on his pad. "And you've been attending sessions with Dr. Rees for a while now?"

Weaver cleared his throat, and for the first time his gait stiffened. "Well, yes. But this really isn't something I'm comfortable discussing."

"I can guarantee you absolute confidentiality. Our only concern is catching the doctor's killer. During your sessions with the doctor, did you gather any details of his personal life?"

"None. He was a professional. He kept to the matter at hand."

"I know it's rather a long shot, but I don't suppose he ever said anything to you indicating that he might be afraid for his life, or that he had enemies?"

"Well, how could he have? He'd scarcely set foot in this country. I should hazard that the only people he encountered were his patients and the others in his household."

"Did you ever meet his daughter?"

"I did. Just bumped into her in the hallway sort of thing. She's a charming young woman," he said, fixing his gaze resolutely away from his wife, before adding, "if a little flighty."

"And did she strike you as someone capable of violence?"

"Listen," said Weaver, leaning forward with elbows propped on his knees, "if there's one thing I learned from my sessions with poor Dr. Rees, it's that anyone is capable of anything."

Mrs Weaver interceded at this point: "My husband has had a lot to cope with recently. His mental health has not been top par."

Weaver cleared his throat. "My wife feels as though she has to defend me. But the truth is, I've come to terms with my limitations. I'm a man with a predilection for solitude. Now, that can be difficult when you have a career like mine. But on the other hand it can have great advantages. Dr. Rees was able to show me that I could reach an agreeable compromise with myself."

"But it's not just misanthropy we're talking about here," Mrs Weaver cut in. "Tell them, Claude."

Weaver sighed. He sat for a moment, collecting himself. "Have you ever heard of a 'fugue state?'"

Flint shook his head slowly, but Spector said: "You mean lost time? Blackouts?"

"Correct." He steeled himself and continued: "This is something I've been experiencing for the past year. And needless to say, it's very concerning."

"Not uncommon, though," Spector observed, "particularly among authors. No doubt you recall Mrs. Christie, who disappeared for eleven days and resurfaced without a memory? That was back in 1926, I think. Around the time she published *The Murder of Roger Ackroyd*. There was some speculation that it was a publicity stunt to promote the book."

"*Ackroyd?*" said Flint. "Yes, I read that one. Thought the whole thing a cheat."

"Really?" said Spector absently. "I'm inclined to think it a masterpiece."

"We are acquainted with Mrs. Christie," said Rosemary. "She and my husband are both quite high-up in the Detection Club."

"How do these fugue states of yours manifest?" inquired Spector, leaning forward as though for the first time taking interest in the conversation.

"It started in January of last year," Weaver explained. "I found myself in Bermondsey with no clue as to how I'd got there. I was *supposed* to be meeting Tweedy then, but obviously I never got there. When I came to, I found a train ticket in my pocket, as well as a matchbook from Robinson's. You know, the gentleman's club. Naturally, I was troubled by this and tried to trace my own movements. But I was unable to do so. I couldn't find anybody who had met me or spoken to me. Those few hours are a blank. They're gone."

"And you've experienced this since?"

"A few times. All perfectly innocuous. Rather like getting blotto and awakening the next morning with a splitting headache. But I don't drink. So these fugue states did a lot of damage to my peace of mind. Not to mention the worry they caused my wife. I couldn't write. Couldn't think. Couldn't travel far or do anything for fear of losing track of myself again."

Flint cleared his throat. "But just to be absolutely clear, sir—you *are* able to account for your whereabouts when the doctor was murdered, I presume?"

Weaver lapsed into the easy good humour that was his typical mode. "I think I can guarantee that, Inspector. My bona fides are exceptional. But then, I'm sure you'll be investigating them thoroughly for yourself."

Flint returned his smile warily. "You can bet on that, sir."

IX

CASE NOTES

"The whole thing is such a mess," said Flint as the pair left the Weaver house, "I'm almost inclined to believe the suicide theory."

Joseph Spector laughed outright. "Oh, the *suicide* theory. It's certainly a creative one, I'll give you that. Not very practical, though. You'll notice how Lidia failed to explain the disappearance of the weapon. Or how the male 'visitor' apparently left the house and did not come back. If the visitor was Rees himself, then how did he get back in the room? He couldn't have gone round to the French window; the downpour was still in force and he would have left a trail of footprints in the mud."

The inspector huffed. "Don't start berating *me*, old man. It's not my theory. But I have to say it's better than anything you or I have come up with so far."

"She does make an interesting point," Spector added thoughtfully, "about this Snakeman. There *is* a certain symmetry between the cases—at least superficially. I'll have to read up on it."

"Here." Flint handed him the leather-bound volume Lidia had lent them. "Take this. *I* certainly have no intention of reading it."

Spector took the book and slipped it inside his jacket.

"Another mystery," Flint continued, "is what the hell Lidia Rees sees in Marcus Bowman. The man's a complete dunce, and smarmy with it."

"Well, I don't suppose we'll ever understand the caprices of the human heart. I am a magician, but no mystery I've ever created has been so enduring and insoluble."

"It's not his bank book, I can tell you that much. Bowman comes from old money, but he's profligate and undereducated. Well, he's an Oxford man, but from my experience there's more to education than just turning up every day. The Bowmans go back a long way. And that trust fund of his has seen him through a lot of problems recently."

"What sort of problems?"

"He's prone to indulgence. You've seen that big yellow car of his? Well, it probably won't surprise you to find out that he is a gambler. Poker is his game. Or rather, it *isn't* his game. He hasn't had a big win in about six months. And his losses are mounting up."

"Hm," said Spector, "in that case his sudden urge to marry a wealthy debutante makes a bit more sense."

"But it still doesn't explain his appeal to *her*. What does he have to offer a woman like Lidia Rees?"

"Defiance against her father, I imagine. He's the vulgar product of a dying upper class. He'd be nowhere without his name. He has no education to speak of, no skill, no wit. He symbolises the polar opposite of her politics and intellect. Do we know how the late Dr. Rees's estate is divided in his will?"

"It isn't. It all goes to Lidia. Everything. The house, the money. The books."

Spector thought about this for a moment. "So if we assume he was killed for the money, that leaves us with one viable suspect."

"But Lidia had no debts. She wanted for nothing."

"*Unless*," posited Flint, "Marcus Bowman's debts are in a worse state than we first thought. Maybe he wants to hasten the marriage so he can get his hands on Lidia's inheritance."

"I doubt she'd fall for a stunt like that, Flint."

"Maybe not. But Marcus has a very high opinion of himself. I don't doubt he also has a tendency to overestimate his own capabilities. Maybe he thought he could convince her that killing her father was the best option for them both."

"A sort of *folie à deux*. Well, stranger things have happened. But what about the alibis?"

"As far as I can tell, each of them provides the other's alibi. It shouldn't be too hard to pick them apart."

The two men were chauffeured by police car to Scotland Yard. On the drive, Flint was quiet and sullen as he stared out the window. Spector had engrossed himself in the book.

This sequence of detailed case studies was the cornerstone of Anselm Rees's psychological reputation. It had first appeared in English in around 1925, in lavish leather-bound editions that were required reading throughout the salons of Paris, London, and any other cultural capitals along the way. Amid the theoretical insight was a gossipy salaciousness concerning the sex lives of the anonymous subjects. For it was well-known that the doctor's patients were all highborn and well educated. Persons of repute and, in some cases, of considerable power. But it was *not* known who they were. Rees had no qualms about sharing the most intimate details of their childhoods and sex lives, but he would never have disclosed their identities. So they were given informal codenames, typically related to the nature of their neuroses. The English translation told of a "Miss Muffet," whose arachnophobia stemmed from an unpleasant childhood incident. And there was "the Tailor's Dummy," a grown man who could not be induced to present himself at the debutant ball because of an incident in his youth when he had been caught trying on his mother's corsets. And then there was Der Schlangenmann.

"I don't see how this Snakeman can be anything to do with the murder," Flint said. He might have been talking to himself. "I mean, we're talking about someone who died years ago, aren't we? Not even English. And besides, how does Lidia know so much about him? She was only ten when it all happened."

"You're forgetting that Lidia was Dr Rees's student as well as his daughter. She studied his failures alongside his triumphs, so you could say that she knows them as well as the late doctor himself."

"But apart from the cause of death (which, I have to admit, is something of a turnup) there really is nothing else to connect the two deaths. It's a different country, a different continent. And it all happened so long ago."

"Yes, you're right. But we're dealing with obsessives, Inspector. You must remember that. And time means nothing to them."

When they got to Scotland Yard, Joseph Spector had finished his reading. As the two men mounted the stairs, he gave the inspector a precis.

"The late Dr. Rees was an excellent writer. Within a few paragraphs he can make you feel as though you were seated within the consulting room yourself. I know a lot about the Snakeman now, evidently more than the poor fellow knew about himself. But I don't know his name. And that's the one piece of information we need if we're to tie the cases together."

"You think there is a link then?"

"Either that, or someone wants us to *believe* there is such a link. But in any case, the more we know about the Snakeman the better."

"Well it strikes *me* that what we're looking for here is an odd one out. Somebody who doesn't quite fit into the scenario. You're absolutely sure about Della Cookson?"

"I can guarantee she was at Benjamin Teasel's house until around eleven. But Teasel's place is in Hampstead, so it would have taken perhaps half an hour for her to get to Dollis Hill by cab."

"Mm." Flint was perplexed. "Then she went straight from a swanky cocktail party to her psychiatrist's house. Presumably making a brief detour to deposit the stolen painting in some secret location. Why did she turn up at Dollis Hill, do you think?"

"No idea. Have you asked her?"

"Of course we've asked her. But I'm asking what *you* think. You have a certain acuity with these things."

Spector smiled. "Kind of you to say. And whether she is the culprit or not, the stolen painting seems to be an entirely different problem altogether. But as for her visit to Rees, maybe it was a prearranged appointment?"

Flint shook his head. "Nothing in the doctor's notebooks to indicate that. Of course, we know he was expecting *someone*."

"Right. You've made the assumption that it was the mysterious, unidentified man who was the doctor's intended visitor all along. When in fact, it may have been *his* visit which was impromptu, while Della was his real appointment from the beginning."

"But surely Rees would have told Olive Turner if Della was his intended visitor?"

Spector shrugged. "Maybe. Maybe not." And that seemed to be the end of the conversation.

"I've been thinking," Flint began, "and it's struck me that the only real odd one out in this whole thing is Marcus Bowman."

"Yes, I see what you mean."

"He's a financier, which is posh talk for saying he doesn't do much of anything. A toff. Spends most of his days boozing and playing golf. His relationship with Lidia Rees is pretty mystifying, but I also find myself wondering what business he has being involved in this saga at all among psychiatrists, artists, and what-have-you."

"Well, I agree that it *is* difficult to understand the attraction he holds for Lidia Rees. Other than a certain youthful folly, that is. I suppose the best guess I can make is that he is the absolute polar opposite of her father. The very antithesis of the stuffy intellectual."

"Exactly." Flint wagged a finger as though his associate had at long last struck on something useful. "Might there be something in that, do you think?"

"Hard to say. I won't know for sure until I meet the man himself."

"Well, you're in luck," said Flint, "because he's waiting for us in my office."

The appointment had been arranged the previous night. Marcus Bowman, who was adamant that he could not remain in the Dollis Hill house under the same roof as a corpse, had been permitted to leave on the condition that he report to Scotland Yard to provide a full statement the following morning. Needless to say, he was not happy with the nine a.m. appointment he had been given and had managed to haggle his way to a twelve p.m. slot. It was twelve thirty when he actually turned up.

He settled himself down in Flint's office, sprawled in a chair as though he owned the place. Flint stood, arms folded, master of his domain. And Spector sat unobtrusively in the corner, riffling a deck of cards. But he took in every word.

"Did you ever meet any of Dr. Rees's patients?" Flint asked. A broad question to get the ball rolling.

"Never had the pleasure. But I'm sure they're an interesting bunch." There was a hint of persiflage in his tone.

"You never bumped into any of them when you were coming and going about the house."

"I'm not sure what sort of ideas you've got, but I never did much 'coming and going' at Dollis Hill. Truth to tell, I don't believe old Anselm ever took to me all that much."

"No? But you did come to the house on a number of occasions since your engagement to Lidia?"

Bowman shrugged. "Mainly to pick her up. Wine-and-dine-her sort of thing, you understand."

"Have you ever met Della Cookson?"

"Della . . . ?"

"Cookson."

"Actress, isn't she? Don't believe so. Saw her in a play the other night, though, now that you mention it."

"She was one of the late doctor's patients. Are you telling me that you never met her at the house on any of your visits?"

Bowman gave another affable shrug. "Tell the truth, old fellow, it's a bit difficult for me to answer you one way or the other. I've no memory for faces, you see."

Flint studied him closely and without sympathy. "What about Floyd Stenhouse?"

"No. Pretty sure I'd have remembered anybody with a moniker like that."

"And how about Claude Weaver?"

"Writer, isn't he? I seem to remember Lidia chattering away about one of his books. Thrillers and bloody murders, isn't it? Maybe you should be asking *him* who killed the poor old man."

"But you never met him?"

"Don't have much of an interest in literature, I'm afraid. Never been much of a reader. Goes all the way back to my days at prep school, I think. They used to try and beat it into you. Makes the whole thing rather unappealing later in life, don't you find?"

"I'm afraid I wouldn't know, sir," Flint answered. But truthfully, he could empathise with Bowman on this point. "Perhaps you'll tell me this, sir: how did you meet Lidia Rees in the first place?"

Bowman settled back into his seat, as though easing into a story he was more than happy to share. "It was in the Palmyra Club, Soho, perhaps you know it? Lively little joint, as the Americans would say. Lovely music."

"You were introduced?"

"More we just sort of bumped into one another. Literally, I think, though my memory's not too good."

"And you're going to be married?"

"In the new year, if all goes well."

"Congratulations." Flint met Spector's gaze and winked. "Now then, can you tell me how you spent last night?"

"We went to the Savoy," said Marcus Bowman. "Marvellous dinner there. Halibut."

"And then what?"

Bowman screwed up his face, making a show of puzzling the whole thing out. "After that we went to the Palmyra. We're regulars there now. A lot of happy memories."

"Aha," said Flint. "How long were you there?"

"Till we came back here. Whatever time that was, I can't be sure."

"And you were together the whole time?"

"Of course we were. Is that some kind of insinuation?"

Flint persisted: "And you didn't stop off anywhere en route?"

"No. We didn't. We took a cab from the Savoy to the Palmyra. And then we took another cab from the Palmyra back to Dollis Hill to drop Lidia off at home and to collect my car."

"I don't suppose you recall the number of the cab which brought you back to Dollis Hill?"

"Now look here, just what is all this about? Somebody did the old man in. And it's all very sad and what-not, but is it really *worth* all this hullaballoo?"

"I'm not sure your fiancée would approve of that sentiment, Mr. Bowman."

"True, she might not," said the young man. Then he added, in a lower tone, as though speaking only to himself: "And then again, she might."

The bar keeper at the Palmyra Club was surprisingly welcoming when Flint and Spector walked through the door. After all, the club itself had played host to many a police raid in its long and storied existence. But the fellow was quick to furnish them with drinks (on the house, of course) and to identify photographs of Lidia Rees and Marcus Bowman.

"Yes, they were here all right," he said.

"What time did they arrive?"

"Couldn't say for sure, but I reckon I must have served them at about ten."

"Did you see them again?"

"Certainly. They were here for a while, no mistaking that. They did some dancing and caused quite a ruckus on the dance floor."

"What sort of ruckus?"

"Oh, you know. A bit of bibulous tomfoolery. Skidding around in spilled champagne, as young people tend to do."

Flint gave Spector a sideways glance. "That doesn't sound like Lidia."

"No, but it *does* sound like Marcus Bowman."

By now it was getting dark. "Come on," said Flint. "I need to get back to the Yard and get my head around all this nonsense. Do you need to be anywhere?"

"Home, I think," said Spector. "I've got some reading to do."

That night, settled in his armchair by the fire at his squat little residence in Jubilee Court, Spector began to read over the notes left behind by Dr. Anselm Rees.

These were not the published case studies, which he had already pored over with interest. There were no snakemen here. These were the handwritten notes the doctor had been keeping since he arrived in London. Their subjects were Patients A, B and C, and once he had deciphered the doctorly scrawl he read the following:

Patient A—a man of prodigious musical talent—is also a man burdened by a powerful sense of guilt. Where does this guilt come from? I can find nothing overt within his recent personal history to have placed this psychological burden on him. Perhaps it is the weight of his immense musical skill (I must confess I am myself an admirer, and possessed several gramophone recordings of his work even before I met him), which has placed this burden upon him. I understand his parents were singularly unremarkable. This makes his role as prodigy all the more astonishing. But he is socially awkward, reclusive, with little in the way of romantic interest (I understand there was once a fiancée who died some years ago, but he is reluctant to discuss this).

The reason he first came to see me was his nightmares—or, as he calls them, his "night demons." I am convinced the key to his trauma lies in these dreams. The focal point seems to be his father, who occurs frequently as a character in said dream-tableaux. But the situations themselves are so outrageous, so bizarre, that they seem almost to defy explanation.

Why should this young man be so different? His brain is a cat's cradle of symbols and ideas. They weave and interconnect, but they are also without beginning or ending. Perhaps putting these dreams in writing will reveal their meaning.

"Clotilde," Spector called out. "Come in here."

His housemaid obliged, and stood patiently while he located a specific passage in the notebook. "Listen to this," he said. He cleared his throat and began to read aloud: "'In the dream I am sitting by a lake. In front of me is an easel and a half-finished canvas. I am painting. It is early morning and there is a light mist on the surface of the water. And suddenly, like a fist in my chest, I feel a sudden thundering dread. I look at my canvas and I realise it is not a picture of the lake at all, but of a hooded figure, bearing a lantern. The figure is watching me from the canvas. And I look up and I see that the lake is changing somehow. Clouds are gathering overhead, and they look so angry. And slowly, from the water, the figure rises. He is holding the lantern, it burns and yet it casts no light. I cannot see his face. But I know he is looking at me. And there is so much fear in my heart.'"

Spector concluded his recitation and snapped shut the notebook. "Well, Clotilde. What do you make of that?"

The maid's face was soft in the ambient fireglow, and yet her expression was intractable. The young woman had been in Spector's service what felt like a lifetime, and in all those years she had never uttered a word.

"That," Spector explained, "was the imaginatively titled 'Dream One' from Dr. Rees's notebook. He ascribes it to 'Patient A,' aka Floyd Stenhouse. What do you make of it?"

But Clotilde, perhaps wisely, remained silent.

In the next section of the notebook, Spector read:

Patient B is a kind of half person. Her mannerisms in social engagements are entirely assumed, as though she has no impulses or authentic reactions of her own. Her only true instinct is that of survival. In this respect one might say she was born to be an actress, that in fact she is never not acting. Behind the convoluted emotional façade is a prurient absence—either that or a wall which is so impenetrable as to subsume all that is recognisably human within her.

This sense of the void manifests literally, in that while she enjoys a life of comfortable means—even luxury—she endures an insurmountable compulsion to steal. She confessed that this proclivity was first apparent in childhood—she recalls snatching a shiny fountain pen from the desk of her schoolmistress, and struggling to hide her glee as the unfortunate teacher searched the desk of every single student. But our Patient B was too canny, even at so young an age. In a moment of distraction, she flung the pen through the open window. The audacity of the crime engendered a perverse admiration in her peers, and she was never called to account. She is full of similar stories of incidents throughout her adolescence and early adulthood. Indeed it appears that her superficial charm has saved her from many scrapes in her life, and needless to say it has provided an invaluable foundation for her career on the stage.

Recently our conversations have tended toward a profound ennui which she is unable to shake off. I understand (though she has not stated so specifically) that there is currently a man in her life. The most salient evidence of this was a single unguarded reference to "we" rather than "I." I have taken to placing small objects around the office during our sessions, not so much to entrap her as to draw her closer to an acknowledgement of the dark side of her nature. In our most recent session I poured a glass of water for her (and one for myself) and as I was placing the glass in front of her I noticed her hand hovering over a gold cigarette lighter I'd left on the glass-topped coffee table. When she realised she was caught, she froze. I asked her what was going through her mind. She looked at me blankly and said simply, "Nothing." Then she withdrew her hand. When the session was over, I noticed that the lighter was gone. I do not know when she took it. More recently I have tried to delve into her past—her family life—to get a better picture of her interpersonal relationships. I must confess I have had little success in this field. But I would like to make note of an incident that occurred during my most recent session with her, which provided an impromptu snapshot of her psyche.

The session itself was over. Patient B, who values her privacy but is not precious on the subject, was about to venture out of my house and into the street. En route, she bumped (and I mean bumped) into a male visitor who was coming to the house. This fellow is a frequent visitor—a suitor of my daughter's—and once he had made his profuse apologies, he looked her square in the face and recognition dawned. "Why, [Patient B]!" He cried, before sputtering out a list of theatrical productions. The fellow has little notion of subtlety, and such a display might easily have reduced a less stolid patient to the corporation of a jelly. But Patient B was diffuse—almost icy—in her approbation. She thanked him politely but with little enthusiasm, before excusing herself and hailing a cab. While my daughter's suitor stood nonplussed, Patient B discreetly withdrew.

But what struck me as interesting about this little encounter was that the man had a gold fob-watch swinging from the pocket of his waistcoat, an ostentatious affectation guaranteed to catch the eye. However, when Patient B climbed into her cab, I saw that my male visitor still possessed the watch. This raises interesting questions about the limits of Patient B's affinity for gold. Why take the lighter (when she had already been caught once in the act of thievery) but not the watch? Perhaps something to do with the fellow's obvious admiration for her, and his knowledge of her past performances on the London stage? What is the correlation between her career and her thievery? This is a question to probe further.

But of course, Rees had not lived long enough to do that.

It was now getting late. Spector closed his eyes a moment and listened to the crackling of the fireplace. There was plenty more reading to do—he had not even reached Patient C yet. But he felt somehow that he was only skirting around the real issue. That the answer to the doctor's murder lay elsewhere. He decided sleep was the best option for him at this point—in the morning, the doctor would still be dead. The painting would still be missing. And the secrets of that locked study would remain as impenetrable as ever.

Monday, September 14, 1936

X

A BRIEF DISQUISITION
ON THE LOCKED-ROOM PROBLEM

O n his way to visit Spector the following morning, Flint stopped off in Bloomsbury where Claude Weaver's publisher, Ralph Tweedy, kept his offices. He did not have an appointment—the mere mention of murder was enough to get him into the esteemed publisher's room.

The fellow was younger than Flint had expected. His face was insufferably smooth. A man, Flint thought, who had achieved nothing on his own merit. A spoilt child, like Marcus Bowman.

"One of your authors is a man named Claude Weaver, I believe?"

The publisher struck a match and ignited the tip of his cigar. "That's right. Claude's one of the very best in the business. Know his work, do you?"

"Afraid not. But don't worry, that's not what my question is about."

"Oh?" Tweedy resumed his seat, cigar clutched between pudgy fingers.

"No. What I want to ask you about is the dinner you had with Mr. Weaver two nights ago."

"Two nights ago? The twelfth, the twelfth . . ." Tweedy said idly. "You'd really be better asking my secretary about that kind of thing."

"We have. In your diary you had a dinner appointment with Claude Weaver. Is that correct?"

"If it's in there, it must be correct," he said, sucking the cigar till the tip glowed orange. "In fact . . . wait a moment. Yes, I do believe I remember it now. Claude wanted to meet me to discuss the contract for his latest novel."

"You met at eight?"

He shrugged: "Thereabouts."

"This was at Brown's?"

"It's where we always meet. Their trout is superb."

"And how long were you together?"

"Oh, a good while." A brief pause, while the smoke coiled upward toward the idle ceiling fan.

"I'll need you to be more specific about that."

The publisher groaned. "Two hours, maybe three hours. Really, this is most unpleasant."

"All I need to know is this—at what time did Claude Weaver leave the restaurant?"

"What time has he told you? Claude has a better memory for these things than I do."

Flint surveyed him through half-lidded eyes. "If I didn't know better, I'd say you were trying to hide something, Mr. Tweedy."

The publisher laughed. "Believe me, that's not my intention." Another pause.

"Did you know Weaver had been seeing a psychiatrist?"

"No I didn't *know* that," the other man responded, "though it doesn't surprise me at all."

"Why not?"

"He's a strange sort, not the easiest to get along with. Writer types, you know. Too introverted. Not in the real world."

"And what did you talk about?"

"Over dinner? The usual. He was nearing the deadline for completion of his latest novel."

"And what's it about?"

The publisher gave a half smile, as though conceding defeat. "A psychiatrist, now that you come to mention it."

"And you talked about it for three hours?"

The publisher sat back, thinking. The only sounds in that office were the creak of the chair, and the sizzle of the cigar. "If you want me to be perfectly honest, no. That was the night Claude was taken ill."

"Ill? This is the first I've heard of this. In what way was he taken ill?"

"Queasy, during the meal. He excused himself, stumbled out to the lavatory and . . . yes, I recall it now. That was the last I saw of him."

"You mean he didn't come back?"

"This wasn't as unusual as it sounds, Inspector. In my business you get used to all kinds of artistic peccadillos."

"What time did he leave?"

"Well, it was halfway through dinner, so probably about ten-ish?"

"Had he complained to you about feeling ill to you before?"

"Not at all. He was talking about the novel, going through a chapter breakdown—which is pretty much the only topic to get him excited about—when all of a sudden he froze, as though maybe he'd seen something over my shoulder. I looked behind me, but there was nothing there."

"Did you say anything to him? Anything that might have been misconstrued?"

"I think what I said to him was . . ." The publisher thought for a moment. "That's it! I was telling him about the new teletypesetter we've got on the shop floor." Off Flint's blank look, he continued: "It's a damn good thing, it'll help us if we ever decide to branch out into paperbacks. But of course, Claude's not what you'd call a fan of the 'popular publishing' boom. That's what we were talking about. It wasn't a heated argument or anything, just a perfectly civil discussion. Claude was trying to convince me that paperbacks were just cheap knock-offs of the real thing. That they might fool the uneducated, but the literati are always going to spot a real Claude Weaver among fakes."

"And that was when he was taken ill."

The publisher nodded. "It's when he got the look on his face. And then he stumbled out of the restaurant, mumbling something about how sickly he felt, and he never came back."

"And this was at ten o'clock?"

"Ten, or half past. I can't be sure."

"Weaver told us that he was with you all evening."

The publisher's smile was insufferable. "Then *Mister* Weaver is mistaken."

⸻

There was a spring in Flint's step has he approached the Weaver residence once again. He had decided Spector could wait a few minutes while he made another house call. This time he did not bother with the bell; he pounded on the door with his fist.

A maid let him in, and before she could protest he marched straight through to the lounge, where he found a bemused-looking Claude Weaver.

"Mr. Weaver, we know you weren't with your publisher for the whole evening the night of the murder. Why did you lie?"

The novelist sprang to his feet. "What are you talking about?"

"He told us that halfway through the meal you were taken ill. You stumbled out into the night and he didn't see where you went."

Weaver looked stricken. "I don't know anything about that."

"We can check with the restaurant staff—"

"No! No, I'm not doubting what you say, Inspector. What I mean is, I have no *recollection* of that."

Flint studied the fellow closely. "What are you trying to tell me, Mr Weaver?"

"I remember the restaurant. I remember the meal. Then I remember arriving home . . ."

"What time was that?"

"I don't know. I went straight to bed."

"So let me get this straight. You're unable to account for your movements the night Anselm Rees died?"

"I-I suppose not."

"And did you visit Anselm Rees at all that night?"

"I don't believe so."

"But you can't say for sure?"

Weaver's jaw clenched and he sat upright, stoical. "No. I can't say for sure."

Flint had no way of knowing it, but Spector had also taken a little detour that morning. He stopped by Benjamin Teasel's place to scope out the missing painting problem. Teasel himself was out, but the two maids who had been on the door the whole evening of the theft were present. Their names were Hilda and Paulette, and they were a comical pair. In their matching uniforms and frilled aprons, they resembled nothing so much as a couple of pepper pots. None of the unostentatious dignity and grace which Spector's own maid, Clotilde, possessed.

"Ladies," said Spector. The two maids looked at each other with ill-disguised smirks. "I would like you to tell me whatever you can about the night of Mr. Teasel's party."

"Certainly, sir," said Hilda, "we'll do whatever we can."

"The master's been most awful upset," Paulette elaborated. "It's getting to be a terrible bind."

"Very well. Then how's about it? The party. Teasel instructed you to admit the guests, correct?"

"Right, sir." That was Hilda. "*We* got the job on account of the fact it was Mr. Townsend's night off." (Townsend, Teasel's valet, had a neat alibi, and was therefore excluded from the investigation.) "Only Mr. Teasel didn't trust one of us to do it on our own, so we paired up."

"I see. And you were in the hall the whole time?"

"Just so, sir." Paulette now. "We let everybody in who had an invite. Everybody who belonged."

"And did you see anybody at all suspicious?"

"No, sir. Nobody. I'm telling you, nobody could have stolen that painting. We didn't let a burglar in, and they proved it wasn't any of the guests, didn't they?"

"You're positive there's no other way the thief could have got into the house on his own?"

"Certainly not, sir. The back door was locked up. So was the side door. All the windows were bolted too."

"Did you see any guests going upstairs at all during the course of the evening?"

"Oh yes! All the time. You see, they had to go up there to use the . . . you-know-what."

"Bathroom?"

Paulette giggled and nodded.

"So it would be impossible for you to say who could have snuck into that room to steal the painting."

"Well, if they came back down with it again we'd be sure to see them," Hilda explained. "And nobody was carrying anything. I can tell you that much for certain."

"Might it have been possible for somebody at the party—one of the guests, I mean—to slip away, unbolt one of the windows to admit the burglar, and then return to the party?"

"No, sir," said Paulette.

"And why not?"

"Because all the other rooms were locked up tight. Mr. Teasel is very particular about people wandering around his upstairs."

"So the only upstairs rooms which were unlocked were—"

"—the you-know-what. That's got a window, but it doesn't open. Never has, not as long as I've been here."

"I see. So it's the stairs or nothing."

"Right you are, sir."

"How about this: could they have got the painting out of the house some other way? Was there another door by which it might have been removed?"

The maids shook their heads in perfect synchronicity. "No, sir. There's only the servant's entrance around the back, and it was locked up tight. Before you ask, all the keys were accounted for."

"So the painting *must* have been carried out via the front door . . ."

"But nobody brought it out past us," Hilda assured him. "I can tell you that for definite."

The maids were keen—perhaps a little too keen—to show him the scene of the crime. They led him up the sweeping spiral staircase to the door at the top. Hilda pushed it open.

"The master keeps it unlocked now," she explained. "He says there's not much point now the painting's gone."

Spector examined the room closely. It was as he had anticipated. The window was, of course, much too small for the painting to have been removed that way. Naturally, it would have been impossible for anybody to climb in or out either.

There was a large window on the landing that looked out onto the street, but it did not open. There was no bolt or latch. The glass was simply affixed into the wall. Another dead end.

In a last ditch attempt to make some sense of it all, Spector headed for the "you-know-what." There was nothing particularly distinctive about the bathroom. No loose fittings or plumbing anomalies that he could see. And, of course, the window was rooted firmly into place by a combination of rust and grime. It would not budge.

Spector descended the staircase frustrated at his lack of progress. He ought to have been abuzz with ideas by now. He collapsed into an armchair in the lounge, and Hilda served him another cup of tea.

"You're working on the death of that doctor too, are you sir?" Paulette inquired delicately. "Quite a case, that is."

"You're right there, young lady. Quite a case indeed."

For the next few minutes the two maids tried in vain to extract a few gory details from him. Spector was reminded of Jonathan Harker in Stoker's *Dracula*, plagued by vampire brides desperate for a drop of blood.

Refreshed by the tea (which was not at all bad), he began to get up from his seat; it was slow and laborious but in the end, with a maid on each arm, he was able to get back on his feet. "I thank you both," he said, touching his brim. "Don't get old, ladies. I doubt it would be to your liking."

All smiles and polite bobs of the head, they showed him out again. He shuddered a little and bundled his cloak tighter around his neat, angular frame.

It was almost lunchtime when Inspector Flint made his return visit to the Black Pig in Putney. He found Joseph Spector in his habitual seat by the window in the snug, this time fiddling with a gold sovereign—imitation, of course. He was twirling it round his gnarled fingers with startling dexterity. So much so that Flint stopped to watch him for a moment rather than interrupt the display.

Then, with a smile, Spector slipped the coin into his pocket. "Please sit down," he said.

"I've got news," Flint told him.

"So have I."

"Me first—Weaver's alibi is shot to pieces. He claims to have suffered one of his 'fugues' while he was having dinner with his publisher. Publisher says he blundered out of the restaurant like he was in a trance."

Spector was chewing his thumbnail thoughtfully. "Yes, I rather thought that might be the case."

"What do you mean? Surely this blows the whole case to bits! If Weaver can't prove his whereabouts, he could easily have gone to Dollis Hill, fugue or no fugue."

"Yes . . . but how did he get into the study?"

Flint opened his mouth, then closed it again.

"I think the time has come," Spector went on, "for us to deconstruct the locked-room problem."

"But what about Weaver?"

"Weaver will wait. If he couldn't even muster a coherent alibi, I find it hard to believe he could have orchestrated this ingenious disappearance from a room which was sealed on the inside."

Flint sighed softly. "You may be on to something there."

Spector began. "Now then, our mutual friend Mr. John Dickson Carr has written a fairly comprehensive study of the locked-room problem in his book *The Hollow Man*. I took the opportunity this morning—as well as a brief sojourn to Benjamin Teasel's place—to reread the relevant section. In it, Carr provides us with seven loose categories. Let's see . . .

"First, death by accident. In other words, if Anselm Rees's throat slashing was the result of an unfortunate mishap.

Perhaps his hand slipped with the letter opener when he was going through the day's post? Unlikely, but not impossible given the right circumstances. All the same I think we can discount it, don't you?

"Second, the victim is induced to kill himself by a drug of some kind. Or hypnotism. While I don't wish to rule it out without comment, and of course you do not yet have the postmortem report on Dr. Rees, I think we can safely say the solution lies elsewhere.

"Third, some sort of mechanical trap is used in the room. A razor blade on a spring, for instance. After a comprehensive search of the room we know we can rule this out. There are no gimmicks or hidden panels.

"Fourth, a suicide rigged up to look like murder. This is the solution Lidia Rees has proposed, so I will not dwell on it further here.

"Fifth, the murderer impersonates the victim *after* having killed him, creating confusion about the time of death. This is possible—after all, Olive Turner only *heard* the doctor through the door after his visitor had left the house. She did not *see* him. And so it may be that the voice she heard was in fact the killer's. But that does not help us to identify the murderer or the visitor, or to explain how the killer was able to vacate the room without a trace.

"Sixth, the murderer manages to attack the victim from *outside* the room. R. Austin Freeman and his Dr. Thorndyke tackled an interesting example of this. But I don't see how this could be applicable to the Rees case. Unless the killer had some kind of bow and arrow, to which a razor blade might be affixed?

"Seventh—and last—the victim is *not* dead at the point when he is discovered. He simply bears the appearance of death. Knocked out or drugged somehow. He is then murdered *after* discovery. Again, this is not possible in our case. Rees was half decapitated, and so there was no question that he was most certainly dead upon discovery. These are the criteria for a locked room, as outlined in Mr. Carr's book."

"Well, where does that leave us?" demanded Flint. He had no idea who this Carr might be, but the fellow sounded as viable a suspect as any in this messy business.

"Food for thought, that's all," answered Spector. "We need to be methodical. As far as I can tell, there are two further complications we need to resolve before we get any further with the locked-room enigma."

"Only two?"

Spector nodded. "The first is the riddle of the impenetrable alibi. There's no such thing as an impenetrable alibi, although some of our key players do come fairly close. We know that Floyd Stenhouse was in his flat. How do we know this? Because the staff can attest that he didn't leave his apartment. There's also the little matter of the telephone call he made to the doctor's study *just before the murder.* This has been confirmed by the telephone exchange and tallies neatly with the fragments of conversation that Olive Turner heard through the door.

"So who's next? Della Cookson. Plenty of witnesses assure us that she most certainly attended her performance of *Miss*

Death, and likewise that she went from there to Benjamin Teasel's house party, at which I was also present. (There's also the little matter of a stolen painting, which we will discuss separately.) We *know* she left the party around eleven thirty, in a state of some distress. We can also surmise that she went from there straight to the doctor's house. She arrived at the front door of the Rees home within fifteen minutes, whereupon she was admitted by Olive Turner. That leaves her little time to get into the house and out again, having committed a gruesome murder without getting so much as a trace of blood on her silk cocktail dress.

"Our third suspect is Lidia Rees. We know she went to dinner at the Savoy, and from there to the Palmyra Club. How do we know this? Because Marcus Bowman tells us so. Likewise, she provides *his* alibi. But not just that—we also have the evidence of the staff at the Savoy, the taxi which deposited the couple at the Palmyra, as well as several club waitresses. I am wont to be wary of couples who are their own alibi, but perhaps we can take their innocence for granted based on the eyewitness testimonies, and the fact that both the Savoy and the Palmyra Club are several miles from the Rees house.

"So: now we come to Claude Weaver, the novelist famed for his fugue-like blackouts. Though he has tried very hard, he has failed to establish a viable alibi. The publisher is unwilling to corroborate, and the wife is unable to do so. This leads us toward an apparently foregone conclusion: that Weaver is the only one who could conceivably have killed Anselm Rees. The evidence is purely circumstantial—there's nothing to indicate enmity between the two men. It is purely that Weaver can't account for his whereabouts the night of the murder. But if he *did* do it (and remember, I say *if*) then that still leaves us with another seemingly insoluble riddle. Namely, how did he get in and out of the house undetected?

"But there's another aspect of this mystery which I've neglected to mention. The mysterious visitor, seen only by Olive Turner, who arrived for an enigmatic final consultation with the doctor. What do we know about this visitor? Only that it was someone Olive had never met before, and who seemed keen to conceal his identity. This was someone the doctor knew, or was at least expecting, because he had told Olive to prepare for a visitor that night. But we don't know what they talked about. All we know is that the visitor left before the murder, and before the telephone call from Stenhouse. So—is the visitor's presence relevant to the murder or not? Apart from Della Cookson, neither of the other two patients was seen arriving or leaving via the front door. Nor was anyone else, save the stranger. This means that the murderer most likely entered the house via the French windows in the doctor's study. But this is impossible for two very distinct reasons: Number one—the rainstorm. The rain began just after nine o'clock—long before the murder—and so there would be a neat set of footprints indicating the assailant's route of ingress. Number two—the French windows were locked on the inside. How do we know this? Because Olive Turner tried them when she entered the room, and so did Della Cookson. Besides that, the key was in the lock on the *inside*. So the killer cannot have entered via that route unless he had a means of erasing his footprints *and* hocussing the lock somehow from the outside. Does that seem like an effective summation of the quandary?"

"It does."

"All right. Let's get down to business. The killer couldn't have left by the door because he would have been seen by both Olive and Della. He couldn't have left via the French windows because his footprints would have been there in the mud for all to see—plus the fact that the windows were locked on the inside.

"We have pinned down the time of the murder to a brief five-minute period between the telephone call from Floyd Stenhouse and the time when Olive broke into the room. Now, greater men than I have discoursed on the locked-room murder, but for our own purposes let me lay out a few basic conceits as they apply to our particular problem. Of course, the whole thing hinges on illusion—the question is determining *where* the illusion lies.

"Point one: the door was not locked at all, but simply *appeared* that way thanks to some trickery. Perhaps it was rigged from outside. This is easier to manage with bolts or latches. For example, we all know the business with the ice cube which, when placed between bolt and catch, slowly melts until the bolt falls neatly into place *after* the murderer has exited the room. Likewise, strings or wires may be used to seal a bolt from outside the room, and then be removed either by severing with a blade, or burning away with a lighter or some such. This isn't possible in our case, because there is no bolt.

This is an old-fashioned "key in lock" scenario. Similarly with the French windows, the key was in the lock. So how could it have been done? Perhaps with a magnet? It bears further investigation.

"Point two: there was some deception concerning time, and the murder was actually committed either before or after the recorded hour. This is, of course, impossible in our case for two reasons. First, we know Rees was alive some moments earlier because we heard him engaged in a telephone conversation with Stenhouse. We have Stenhouse to corroborate this. And of course he could not have been killed after because there is no mistaking a razor death. The only means it *might* have been done is if a recording was used to imply that Rees was alive when in fact he had been killed some time before. But we have both the telephone records (which establish the time and duration of the call) *and* Stenhouse's testimony (which establishes that Rees was *alive* at the time in question). And apart from that, there is no sign of any recording equipment within the room which may have been used to bring about such a trick. All the same—food for thought.

"Point three: perhaps the murderer never left the room at all? Stranger things have happened. And we all know about the infamous wooden chest which would easily take a human body. But of course, the chest was opened by Olive, and it was established that there was no one in there. The room was empty. So just where did he go?

"This brings us to point four: what if he was never in the room at all? It has been known for murders to be triggered within a locked room from some external location. Typically this would be a firearm-related death, for example, where an inanimate pistol is remotely triggered. I'm thinking particularly of a tale by Melville Davisson Post—perhaps you know the one? This would be nigh-on impossible with the method used to kill Rees. It was a very personal attack, very physical. This is not a crime which could have been somehow automated. Figuratively speaking, there are human fingerprints all over it.

"But point five offers us a potential solution: what if the victim was somehow impelled to kill himself? It could be done with some trickery. If, for example, the victim walked into a booby trap which strangled him or stabbed him. A spring-loaded dagger, for instance. Remember Wilkie Collins and that strange bed of his. Or even if it was no murder at all, but a bewildering instance of suicide which has been mistaken by witnesses for a murder? A man could conceivably slice his own throat with a razor. If he was angry or demented enough, he might even do the kind of damage that Rees suffered. But that leaves us with yet more crypticities. If Rees killed himself, what happened to the weapon? We know that the weapon was a razor, and razors are made of metal. And we cannot escape the fact that the room was searched and no razor, or trace of a razor, was found."

"Well there you have it," said Flint, "you've laid out the problem. Now how's about offering a solution?"

"The principle of Occam's razor states that the solution requiring the least amount of guesswork is most likely the correct one."

"And what solution is that?"

Spector's smile was vulpine. "Let's continue to look at it methodically." He dealt out three cards facedown. Then he turned over the first card to reveal the Queen of Hearts. "Della Cookson. No motive to speak of. But she was present at the scene of the crime, and we know there's something she is trying to hide from us."

He turned over the next card: the Jack of Diamonds. "Floyd Stenhouse. Motive: uncertain. But he had no opportunity, because we've established an alibi for the time of the murder."

Then the final card: the King of Clubs. "Claude Weaver. Motive: uncertain. But he had the opportunity, and he already lied to us once about his whereabouts the night of the murder. Ah! But of course," he suddenly exclaimed, producing a pair of cards from his breast pocket, "I'm forgetting something."

He placed these two additional cards beside the others, revealing them to be a pair of jokers. "We have our jokers, Marcus Bowman and Lidia Rees. They provide their own alibis, but at the same time Olive Turner would have known immediately if either of them had been in the house that night. Besides, we know they were on the other side of London at the time it all happened."

"Did you ever think," Flint cut in, "that maybe Olive Turner might be covering for Lidia?"

"For what reason? This isn't some old family retainer we're talking about. Olive had been working in the Rees household for only a matter of months. She had no ties to Lidia, at least nothing which might justify shielding her from a murder charge. No, no, Flint—these are our jokers. They are anomalies. And of course, last but by no means least . . ." He shoved a hand deep into his trouser pocket and emerged with one final card. He placed this beside the jokers. It bore no suit, simply a copperplate question mark. "We have our faceless visitor, whom nobody has seen since or managed to identify."

He scooped up the six cards and began to shuffle them.

XI

SNAKEMAN UNMASKED

W hen the two men parted company a little later, Flint was evidently dispirited at the outcome of Spector's lecture. But Spector himself seemed suddenly enthused. He told Flint he was heading to the Pomegranate to try and get some information out of Della Cookson. This was, however, a half-truth; on the way over there he stopped by the Rees house for a quick consultation with Lidia.

She had taken up residence in her late father's office, and she was sitting behind his desk when Olive Turner ushered Spector in. She wore a pair of thick bottleglass spectacles as she pored over a large volume.

"Good afternoon, madam," said Spector, discreetly scanning the room. The pool of blood, he noticed, had been covered by a discreet mohair rug.

"Mr Spector," she said, barely looking up from the book. "Please sit down."

Spector settled himself on the couch and said: "I would like to ask your professional opinion on something, Miss Rees."

"Go on."

"I would like you to tell me about 'fugue states.'"

Whatever she had been expecting, it was clearly not this. She thought for a moment.

"A fugue state is a fragmentation of the memory. A distancing between oneself and one's consciousness. From the individual's point of view, he may have blacked out entirely and simply come to once again at the right moment."

"Could this hypothetical fellow do things in a fugue state which he would not do in his waking life?"

"Certainly. Go anywhere. Do anything."

"Could he commit a crime?"

"Oh, easily. He could do anything. Anything at all."

"What else do you know about the affliction?"

"Well, it remains something of a mystery. Typically it stems from childhood coping mechanisms. A child who is troubled will devise a means of separating himself from the events in question, of convincing himself that these events are happening to somebody else. And eventually, this will become the truth. His personality—his very *self*—will splice. He will slip into this almost trancelike state, during which time he will have no knowledge whatsoever of his actions."

"So if your father was killed by a man in a fugue state, you're saying the fellow couldn't be held accountable?"

"No. Because, you see, it was scarcely him at all. It was somebody else. A kind of phantom stranger within his skull."

Spector ruminated. "It's a frightening thought."

"Mm. But imagine how frightening it is for the man himself. To know that all these things are happening, that you are the one responsible, but that you have no free will to control them."

"So a man may conceivably commit murder in one of these fugue states?"

She looked at him closely, with the aspect of seeing him truly for the first time. "A man may do anything," she said.

"And what can you tell me about dreams?"

"Floyd Stenhouse's dreams, you mean? I assume you've been reading my father's notes."

"I have indeed. A dream, your father states, is like a poem. It invents and reinvents its own language. It's lyrical, ambiguous. And most importantly, it never quite gets to the point. So a dream is the pursuit of clarity, the unpeeling of images and symbols. With that in mind, what do you make of Floyd Stenhouse's dreams?"

"My father developed criteria for decoding dreams. Firstly, he posited a superficial, filmic layer that he called the 'tangential continent.' These are aspects with exact correlations in the waking world. So, for instance, a student about to undergo examination will experience dreams about said examination beforehand. But beneath that initial layer is a second layer, which he termed the 'meaty corpuscle.' This is the realm of the symbols. Where a person's waking life and behaviour diverges significantly from the instinctual unconscious, the meaty corpuscle becomes more pronounced. The dreams assume an allegorical, imagistic aspect. That is the case with Mr. Stenhouse."

"And what about his dreams, specifically? How do you interpret them?"

"There's only one way to interpret them: symbolically. For instance, a lamp signifies illumination, the uncovering of a secret. Teeth are violence. Water is aging, the ravages of time. So a man, Stenhouse's father, holding a lamp, rising from a still lake seems to represent the resurgence of a figure from the past. A secret revealed. And the jaws—violence, consumption."

"And what does it tell you about Stenhouse himself?"

Lidia was deathly serious as she removed her spectacles. "Mr. Spector, Stenhouse is not my patient. I've had no hand in diagnosing him. I believe the only man who could have conceivably answered your question is my father."

Spector considered this. After a moment's silence, he said: "And what about your own dreams, Dr. Rees?"

"I have no dreams."

"None? But you have such an active mind."

She interlaced her fingers thoughtfully. "Let's say I am . . . incapable of dreaming."

Another lengthy pause as Lidia and Spector studied each other like duellists. "Forgive my impertinence," said Spector, "but did you love your father?"

"That's rather like asking the Earth if it loves the sun."

"Is it?"

She peered at him over the rims of her spectacles. "Like God, Anselm Rees made me in his image."

"You sound bitter."

"I am as incapable of bitterness as I am of dreaming." Her face was completely without expression.

—·—

Two days into his investigation, Inspector George Flint got his first and only piece of good luck. He had resigned himself to a lengthy and circuitous campaign of digging around to identify the Snakeman. When he got back to Scotland Yard, however, he was greeted by an unusually chipper Sergeant Hook.

"I know that smirk, Hook. Seems like you've stumbled on something."

"I have indeed, sir," answered the sergeant.

The fact was that when Anselm Rees emigrated from Vienna to London, he had ordered his archive of papers to be brought with him. This meticulously maintained catalogue of handwritten records was currently at Oxford University, waiting to be integrated into the Bodleian's vast library of psychiatric tomes.

"I was a bit worried, sir," said Hook, "because I was afraid the only source would be the patient records at the Wachau Valley clinic. Now they'd have been hard to come by on a good day, but it turns out most of the records were destroyed in a fire a few years ago. But it *also* turns out that Dr. Rees maintained his own private set of records. So in the end all it took was a little cross-referencing. I just had a cable through from Vienna confirming the death records."

"And?"

"The Snakeman's real name was Bruno Tanzer."

"Bruno Tanzer." Flint rolled the name around on his tongue. "And what have we found out about Tanzer?"

"Only what I could get from the Viennese authorities. Tanzer had a wife, but she died in a flu epidemic. She did, however, give him a daughter. Born 1900. Which would make her—"

"—thirty-six," Flint supplied. "There's only one woman in this case who could conceivably fit the bill for the Snakeman's daughter, and that's Della Cookson." He grinned at the sergeant. "Hook, once again you have excelled yourself. Keep plugging away, see what else you can find out. I'm going to the Pomegranate Theatre."

When he arrived at the Pomegranate, Joseph Spector came across Benjamin Teasel alone in the bar. The producer was gazing forlornly into a pink gin. He seemed to have aged a few decades since he lost his painting, but at the sight of Spector, he leapt to his feet.

"Joseph! Any news old man?"

"News?"

"Yes, news! *El Nacimiento*! What did you think I was talking about? I need you to work your magic for me Joseph."

"You know I'll do what I can for you, Benjamin. But you have to remember that a man has died. A famous man at that.

Such events tend to enliven the public imagination rather more than the theft of a painting."

"That's why I'm asking *you*," Teasel went on with a forced, saccharine sense of playfulness. He draped an arm around Spector's cloak-clad shoulder. "I know you of all people are quite capable of resolving both incidents at a fell swoop. And do you *honestly* believe there is any chance at all that Della stole the painting and did *not* also kill her doctor?"

"That's . . . interesting," said Spector. "Do you have any basis for that argument?"

"Spector, I don't have *anything*. All I know is that I made the stupid, foolish, and downright asinine error of showing that wicked woman my latest acquisition. She was the only one who knew it was there, and she was the only one who could possibly have snagged the keys from around my neck."

"Now Benjamin," chided Spector, "*neither* of those statements is true. I've been to your parties before, and I know how thick the alcoholic haze can get. It's hard to tell where one guest ends and another begins. Someone else could easily have got hold of those keys."

"Well," Teasel said with a note of resolution, "you'll have to find out won't you?"

Not long after that, Inspector Flint exploded into the foyer and approached the pair at the bar. "Spector, I need to talk to you."

Spector excused himself and went off with Flint. The two of them made their way discreetly backstage, while Flint detailed the discovery of the Snakeman's real identity.

"So the Snakeman has a daughter," said Spector, lighting a cigarillo. "Do you really believe it's Della?"

Flint produced his notepad and studied it.

"Della Cookson," he read. "Given name, Mabel Norman. No birth records in existence, but we have it on good authority she was previously a resident at the Oak Tree Home for Unwanted Infants. An orphan, in other words. When she came of age, she first worked as a maid in the Plaza Hotel. And from there to the chorus of the Belmont Follies. The rest, as they say, is history."

"So she *might* be the Snakeman's daughter?"

"It's a possibility. And the closest we've got to a lead in terms of motive."

"Doing some detecting are you, *Mister* Spector?" It was Lucy Levy who had spoken. She was leaning her back against the brick wall, supine like a cat.

Spector turned to her. "I am, as it happens. Why? Have you got something you want to tell me?"

She laughed. It was a studied, theatre-school laugh. "There's a lot of mysteries in this theatre, aren't there? Poor old Benjamin loses his painting. Della Cookson of all people snags the lead in this horrid little play. And then, of course, there's Edgar Simmons."

"Edgar Simmons?" Spector knew the name. He had heard it before. But where? "Who's Edgar Simmons? You'll have to enlighten me, Lucy."

"Just another mystery for you to solve," she said, slinking away. Perhaps she wanted him to follow, but Spector wasn't in the mood. He stood and watched her go.

When they got to the star dressing room, Della Cookson was already in full costume. She studied herself in the mirror and scarcely acknowledged their arrival. "Gentlemen," she said icily. "What can I do for you?"

"We're just here to wish you luck, Della. And to ask you one or two questions."

Flint stepped forward. "Tell me please, Miss Cookson, if you have ever heard the name 'Snakeman?'"

She looked at them, blinking. "The name means nothing," she said.

"Take a moment to consider. Snakeman was a pseudonym given to a German psychiatric patient by the name of Bruno Tanzer."

The actress shook her head.

"Tanzer died by his own hand. He killed himself in the autumn of 1921. Think very carefully. Are you sure you have no knowledge at all of Bruno Tanzer?"

"Gentlemen, I've no idea what you are talking about."

"All right," said Spector resolutely. "It was a slim hope, I suppose. How are you feeling about tonight's performance?"

"Fine, thank you Joseph. You know me. When I'm onstage, *everything* is fine."

Taking his cue from Spector, Flint put in: "It must take a lot out of you."

Della sighed. "Acting. It's such a transient existence at the best of times. Take Edgar Simmons—you remember him, Joseph? Just last week we were talking at the Ivy and he was telling me how things were finally looking up for him, he was onto a nice cushy little number, a regular gig, and the *next* thing I hear he's taken flight, gone abroad somewhere. And in *quite* a hurry, I understand."

"Simmons? Lucy Levy mentioned him just now. Who is he?"

"Edgar? Oh, just a middle-aged actor. One is very much like another, don't you find?"

"But he disappeared?"

She let the question dangle tantalisingly. "'Disappeared' is such a melodramatic term."

"Do you prefer 'vanished'? He's gone, is that what you're trying to say?"

She looked at him with an aspect of divine patience. It would have suited her in that moment to play a nun. "Yes, Joseph. That is precisely what I'm trying to say."

"And when did you last see him?"

"Oh, a week ago perhaps. He was one of the faces one sees about the place. And then, all of a sudden, he wasn't."

Spector smiled. "Hot-footed it, you think? One of his dolly birds must have a husband."

"Could be. But really, I'm just saying that we theatre folk don't have anything we can really rely on. Nothing tangible. You might be riding high when you step offstage, and then the next day you're on the scrapheap. It can happen that quick."

"Is there something you want to talk about, Della?"

"No," she guffawed, "I'm just getting maudlin. Funny how murders seem to do that to me."

"You've got a phenomenal career with many years onstage ahead of you. You have nothing to be afraid of."

Della looked at him, smiling, and said nothing.

On the dressing table, Flint spotted a dog-eared book. The legend on the spine read *THE BLOOD RITE by Claude Weaver*.

"Do you know Claude Weaver?" he asked, pouncing on the book.

"Mm? No, no. Just an admirer. Why?"

There followed an awkward pause, before Spector said: "Claude Weaver was one of Dr. Rees's other patients."

"Well," said Della, unfazed, "fancy that. No, I never met him."

"What about Floyd Stenhouse?" asked Flint.

Her gaze snapped toward them. "Floyd? What about Floyd?"

The inspector's brow furrowed. "You know him, then?"

"We go back a long way. I wouldn't say I *know* him, exactly . . ."

"But you'd met him before?" said Spector soothingly.

"Not recently . . ."

"When?" Spector continued.

"When we were young."

"So you were childhood friends? What was he like, when he was young?"

"I couldn't tell you. We weren't close."

Sensing that he had exhausted this line of inquiry, Spector took a step toward Della. "I'm going to teach you a little magic now," he said with a smile, "if you'll permit me."

Della blinked at him.

"Here," the old man went on. He grasped and brought down from a wall-mounted cupboard three white mugs, identical in design. He lined them up side by side on the tabletop. He produced from his pocket a small red rubber ball. He flicked it across the room to Della, who caught it in her sleekly manicured hands.

"Place the ball under one of the mugs," he instructed. She lifted the middle mug and put the ball under it.

"Now," he went on, turning his back, "I want you to fool me."

For perhaps twenty seconds, Della moved the mugs around. Spector—with his back turned and his eyes closed, could hear the scraping of the porcelain against the mahogany surface. Flint watched all this without a word.

Then: "All right," Della said.

Spector turned to face her and did not smile. His face scarcely moved as he spoke. "You are satisfied that there is no way I can know which mug the ball is under? I could not possibly have seen?"

Della nodded.

"Then prepare to be amazed," he said, springing forward and lifting the mug on the left, revealing the rubber ball. "You think, perhaps, it was blind luck? Very well. Let's repeat the experiment, shall we?"

They did so twice more, with Spector facing the wall and Della swapping the mugs around. Each time, Spector found the ball.

"Like every single mind-reading act," he explained, "it's just a hoary old fraud. When I picked up the mugs I noted that although they were exactly the same shape and design, each possessed a certain *something* to distinguish it from its fellows. This one here has a minute chip in the rim. This one has a hairline crack in the handle. And the underside of this one is ever so slightly discoloured, as though it had been left upturned in the sun for too long. Scarcely visible to the naked eye—particularly in the dim light of the dressing room—but if you train yourself you can spot these things quite readily. And if it were not these particular details, it would have been something else.

"Anyway, I angled them to minimise the chances of your spotting each imperfection. I stood so that my shadow fell across the faded mug; even if you noticed the discolouration, your eye would convince your brain the shadow was responsible. And I simply turned the chipped rim and cracked handle so that they faced me. When I asked you to place the ball beneath one of the mugs, the innate psychological desire for symmetry dictated that you would place it under the middle one. If you hadn't it would not have mattered. I knew exactly where the ball was at all times. Of course, I could not entirely rule out the notion that you might spot one or other of these minuscule flaws when you were moving the mugs around. But I am an artist: I was willing to take the risk.

"So there you have it. Satisfied?"

"Not really," Della said. "It's such a drab solution. I was hoping for something rather more exciting."

"But that's all magic is, my dear. Taking the mundane and making it remarkable. And still, the trick teaches us something about perception. No matter how deceptive you *thought* you were being, my view was always clearer than yours. You may have thought you were tricking me. But of course, all along *I* was tricking *you*."

She gave him a smile but it was somehow hard and humourless. It did not reach her eyes.

On their way out of the Pomegranate, Flint paused to murmur in Spector's ear: "Why did you make such a hullaballoo about Edgar Simmons? I've never heard his name before."

"I'm always wary of names which occur multiple times in different contexts. . ."

"Don't get distracted, Spector," Flint warned. "Your main business is Anselm Rees. Don't forget that. I don't want you heading off down a dead-end alley of some disappearing actor. Surely actors disappear all the time?"

"Oh, they most certainly do," Spector was quick to agree. "But usually when they disappear, no one remembers them."

They took a brief detour via the stage, where Lucy Levy was running through some lines. They were not her lines, but Della's. Evidently she had set her heart on snagging the lead.

"Miss Levy. Forgive me for interrupting, but I have a question. You seemed very keen for me to take an interest in Edgar Simmons. Do you have anything you'd like to tell me?"

She gave him a *who, me?* wide-eyed look. "I hear you like mysteries, that's all."

"You tell me he disappeared. Della Cookson said the same thing. When did this happen?"

"Oh, I don't know. He was here one day and then the next day . . . he wasn't."

Spector turned to Flint. "Do you think you could find out an address for Edgar Simmons?" Flint gave him a look. "I know, I know. 'Don't get distracted.' But certain individuals are *very* keen for me to take an interest in Mr. Simmons. That can't be a coincidence, can it?"

Flint opened his mouth to tell the old conjuror that it most certainly could be coincidence and in fact almost certainly was, but he stopped himself. It was no use trying to argue. Instead he just agreed and wrote down the name of the vanished actor in his notebook.

<hr />

When they got back to Scotland Yard, Flint poured out two glasses of scotch in his office so that the two men might settle down to dissect the day's discoveries.

"I think," Spector commenced, "that we may be getting too caught up on the idea that Della is involved. I've no doubt that she's lying to us about something. But I mean, we've no proof as yet that she's the Snakeman's daughter."

"You're right," Flint ruminated between sips of scotch. "Here is a thought. Now bear with me, because it may seem a little strange. But what if the Snakeman didn't commit suicide at all? What if he was murdered?"

"Well, the reports concerning the death *are* sketchy. It would be easy enough to disguise a murder as a hysterical suicide. But it limits the number of suspects, doesn't it? I mean, if we assume Della isn't Tanzer's daughter, there's no way any of the doctor's current patients could have been involved."

"No. But . . . there *is* a way Lidia could have been involved."

"But she was so young! Barely ten, wasn't she, when Der Schlangenmann died?"

"Some children," Flint said sagely, "are born bad."

"So let me get this straight. You're telling me that Lidia Rees—at ten years old—snuck into her father's sanitarium and slashed the throat of one of his patients? A grown man?"

Flint's reasoning was, it must be said, logical. "A grown man who was sedated out of his mind. Children have been known to commit much more outlandish crimes than this."

"But if what you're saying is true, then why would Lidia draw attention to this monstrous crime of hers? Why even mention it to us at all?"

"You said it yourself, Spector. What we're dealing with is abnormal psychology."

"But she has an alibi."

"Who, Bowman? He's a buffoon. Scarcely knows what day it is. He'll say whatever she tells him to."

"That's true enough. But then we have the testimonies of the staff at the Savoy to contend with. Plus the few bystanders at the Palmyra."

"Look," said Flint, growing impatient, "I don't know *how* she did it. But this whole thing smacks of a killer who's too clever by half. Who's not scared to dangle the truth under our noses because she thinks we'll never be bright enough to spot it."

Spector leaned back in his seat. "I don't disagree with you, Flint. We're talking about a brazen killer who's not afraid of being caught. Someone who no longer values his or her own life. And people like that are always the most dangerous." He met the inspector's eye: "Take care, Flint. Tread carefully."

They finished their drinks, and Spector bade Flint good night. It was dark outside now, but Flint watched the old man via the window as he hailed a cab and disappeared into the encroaching evening. It was then that the inspector became conscious of someone loitering sheepishly behind him, in the office doorway.

"What do you want, Hook?"

"Bit of bad news, sir." He could not quite meet the inspector's eye.

"And what's that?"

"It's Bruno Tanzer's daughter, sir. I happened to overhear part of your conversation, and I'm afraid it's a no-go. She died in 1929, in Berlin."

Flint exhaled ruminatively. "How did she die?"

"Suicide. I'm afraid she slashed her throat."

Flint closed his eyes and rubbed his palm aggressively over his forehead. "So that's where the trail ends."

"I'm sorry, but it looks that way."

"Tanzer had no other relations, or even any connections, that we can trace."

"I'm sorry I can't give you better news, sir. I know you were holding your hopes up for this one."

After a beat, Flint said: "Not your fault, Hook. I'm going home. Need a good night's rest to get my thoughts in order. I'd advise you to do likewise. But do me a favour first, will you? On the way home, stop by Joseph Spector's place and give him the bad news, eh?"

Jerome Hook was the fifth of his line to work in furtherance of law and order. It was all he had ever known, and all he was likely to know. When (God willing) he had a son, he would no doubt bestow that same knowledge on the little one too. He ate, slept, and breathed in edicts and dictats. But he had never in his twenty-five years met anyone like Joseph Spector. Or, for that matter, visited anywhere quite like the house in Jubilee Court.

Clotilde the maid was an angular girl of about twenty, with pale porcelain skin and auburn hair ornately coiled round her head. Her face was impassive as she surveyed him on the doorstep.

"I was looking for Mr Spector," he said, scuffing his feet on the cobbles and not quite knowing what to do with his hands. She did not speak, but bobbed her head slightly and stood aside to let him pass through into the house.

So this was what the inside of a magician's house looked like. The hallway was nondescript enough—oak-panelled and dimly lit by dust-caked gas lamps—not all that dissimilar from the Rees house. But when she led him through to the study, it was like stepping into another world.

"Ah!" Spector cried with what appeared to be genuine delight at the sight of Hook. "Welcome to my sanctum sanctorum."

The room was amazing. The walls were papered with old variety posters, many of which included somewhere on the bill "The Spectacular Mr. Spector." It was a torrent of colour, like stepping into the old man's weird brain. The shelves were crammed with books, of course, but this study was also apparently a museum or a trophy room, filled with strange and wonderful humbugs. A Fiji Mermaid in a tall glass jar, pickled in yellowish fluid; a row of shrunken heads, threaded together ear to ear in a ghoulish chain; various clockwork gewgaws; a spirit cabinet hung with plush velveteen curtains. Tarot cards and other mad occult trappings. Absurdly, there were also a pair of incense burners that gave the room a musty and also somewhat threatening patina of mist, as though some dark rite was about to take place.

"Mind Tom Thumb's bones," said Spector. Hook, bemused, almost blundered into a tiny skeleton hung on a wire frame beside the door like a boot scraper.

The two men sat by the fire. Spector looked somehow stranger in the firelight, waxy and not quite real at all. He must have known it suited him. "Tea, Sergeant? Or can I tempt you with a more adventurous concoction?"

"Tea will be fine," said Hook. It was a battle to keep the insipid adolescent squeak from his voice. He just about managed it.

"Clotilde," said Spector. He was looking at the silent maid. She bobbed again and left the room. "Now what can I do for you?" he said to Hook. "It must be an emergency, if the inspector sent you out here for me."

"Some bad news, sir. Della Cookson isn't the Snakeman's daughter."

"How do you know?"

"Because the Snakeman's daughter killed herself back in 1929."

Spector thought about this. "I see. Well, I suppose it makes sense. I imagine the inspector is rather disheartened. I, however, am not. You see, this is a case with many facets. Almost too many. Take this, for example."

He turned in his seat and switched on the gramophone at his side. It evinced the sound of a lone violin; piquant, hopeful, drifting like a dove over scenes of dread and carnage.

"Floyd Stenhouse," said Spector. "Isn't he wonderful?"

"Very talented," Hook said with an embarrassed cough.

"Of course we know that genius and madness go hand in hand. History tells us so. And I gather from Rees's notes that Mr. Stenhouse is a man plagued by torments of the unconscious. He has dreams—hideous dreams. Monstrous dreams, to rival the darkest imaginings of Edgar Allan Poe. Listen to this:"

He reached out and lifted the needle from the gramophone. No diminuendo: silencing the music with an abrupt squawk. Then he turned his attentions to the notebook. "Here is an entry dated two weeks ago. 'In the dream, Patient A is in bed as usual, writhing with fever. The sweat oozes from his body, and he is convulsed by a twisting pain in his gut. Gradually, he comes to realise that he is not alone. Silhouetted by the moonlight beyond the bedroom window, he sees a figure dressed in black. And he knows that this figure—whomever it might be—is the cause of his agony. His instinct is to lash out, to strike at the person responsible for such pain. He seizes something from the table beside his bed and hurls it at the figure. Instantly, the figure vanishes in a cascade of shattered glass. And Patient A realises that he has only shattered a mirror.'"

"All this stuff means nothing to me, sir."

"No? You mean you don't find it interesting? Not even in the slightest?"

"Feels like voyeurism. A man's dreams are his own business."

"I'm sure you're right about that. And yet Mr. Stenhouse seems only too eager to share his dreams. So eager, in fact, that he telephoned Dr. Rees in the middle of the night to describe his latest nightmare while it was still fresh in his mind. Evidently Dr. Rees himself found a lot of interest in the night terrors of this troubled musician. Perhaps he foresaw another bestseller in the making."

"What are you getting at, sir?"

"Answer me one question, Hook. What was Dr. Rees's immediate reaction when Stenhouse began reciting the content of his dream?"

"He started writing it down. Olive Turner heard the pen scratching on paper."

"Correct! He immediately began to make notes. Now answer this: what *happened* to those notes?"

Hook was stumped. "The latest notes were the ones he was making before Olive took him his supper. We didn't find anything subsequent to that."

"Which implies what? That the killer perhaps tore the relevant page out of the notebook? That perhaps there was something *else* on that page which he did not wish us to see?"

"But *why*?"

Spector grinned. "I think at last we may be asking the right question."

When he got home, Inspector George Flint found himself somewhat distracted. His wife placed a bowl of stew in front of him, which he devoured in between monosyllabic grunts. Julia Flint was a patient woman and knew not to expect too much of her husband when he was so immersed in a case. But even she was a little nonplussed by his vacant, glassy stare as he sat by the fireside in the dimly lit lounge.

It was not long before he dozed off in his chair, his fingers knotted across his belly. Julia came back into the room bearing a pot of coffee, but when she saw him asleep, she tutted once and went to bed alone.

Flint, slumped down in the chair in an unconscious echo of Anselm Rees's death pose, began to snore. But his seemingly peaceful sleep was troubled.

He found himself in a doorless, windowless room. No possible means of entrance or exit. The place was familiar, and yet somehow fearsome. There was an uncanny menace to it. He looked around him. He scoured the walls for some trick panel or hidden compartment. On the far side of the room, he spotted a man-sized wooden chest. With a pang of fear, he gripped the arms of his chair and heaved himself to his feet.

"Doctor," said a voice. It was a woman's voice, and yet it was tinny and mechanical, as though it were drifting from an invisible gramophone. "Doctor?"

What is it? he tried to say, but his throat produced no sound.

"Doctor . . ."

He approached the chest, slowly.

"Doctor. There is a visitor for you."

His hand hovered over the lock on the chest. As he was poised to open it, to his surprise it clicked open of its own accord. With a creak, the lid swung upward. And a figure began to rise from the chest.

With a voiceless gasp, Flint stepped backward. The figure—an agglomeration of formless shadows—rose up until it towered over him. His eyes could not quite focus, but he made out a man in a coat and a hat.

"Who are you?" he tried to say.

"Doctor," repeated the disembodied female voice, "there is a visitor for you."

Flint felt the familiar dread rising in his chest. With gloved hands, the shadow-creature reached out to him, and as it did so, its face came slowly into focus. It was not a human face. It bore twin rows of fierce sharp teeth, flecked with blood and bile. Its eyes were beady and black. It was the face of a man-sized snake.

With a priapic jolt, Flint woke. The fire had burned to nothing, and morning sunlight streaked through the curtains of the lounge. He sat up, panting, and was distressed to find that his sweat had soaked through his shirt. He got to his feet slowly, like an old man. His knees shook as he stumbled out to the kitchen for a glass of water.

PART THREE
THE
IMPOSTOR'S TALE
(SEPTEMBER 15–17, 1936)

"It is funny, isn't it?" asked Bruce. "It *is* funny. All the time I was trying to get the goods on you, everybody thought you were trying to get the goods on me."

"I have a knack," said Bewlay with perfect seriousness, "of arranging things like that."

—Carter Dickson, *My Late Wives*

It isn't that they can't see the solution. It is that they can't see the problem.

—G. K. Chesterton, "The Point of a Pin"

ENTR'ACTE (II)

MISTER WEAVER MAKES A

PURCHASE

M orrison's Hardware was a small establishment in a row of shopfronts along the Portobello Road. Its large square window was crowded with ironware, mangles, a clotheshorse, fishing rods, Swiss army knives, and other such ephemera. The proprietor, Morrison himself, had scarcely turned the sign on the door to OPEN when Claude Weaver tumbled in from the street. Weaver looked wan and dishevelled, but when he approached the counter his manner and speech were perfectly composed. He spoke crisply, and with authority.

"I want *that*," he said, indicating an object in a glass case on the wall behind the counter.

"And good morning to you too, sir," Morrison answered.

"Quick about it," said Weaver, examining his pocketwatch.

Without a word, the elderly proprietor unlocked the case and extracted the item. Henry Morrison held no truck with discourtesy, and was happy to take as long as necessary. He took his time about getting the cabinet open, and as he did so he took the opportunity of getting a good look at this rather extraordinary fellow who had burst in from the street at dawn. He was pale skinned and bald headed, and the skin about his neck and jowls hung limply, as though he had recently lost a bit of weight.

"And what might sir be wanting with an item like this?"

"What do you think? Protection! I need it to protect myself."

The shopkeeper leaned forward, delighting in this unexpected slice of melodrama. "Got enemies, have you?"

"Are you going to sell me a revolver or not?" snapped Weaver.

But the fellow was already ringing up the purchase on his till.

XII

THE VAMPIRE TRAP

September sixteenth drifted by in a haze of undirected industry. Everybody was working, even Spector (though you would be hard-pressed to tell what he was doing). In fact, the old man spent a good hour hobnobbing with actor types in the various pubs and bars along the Strand. They had much to tell him of the missing actor, Edgar Simmons.

"Such a dear," said Mavis Le Fley over her second pink gin, "but he *had* been rather full of himself lately."

"In what way?"

"Well, when we reach a certain age, darling, it *can* get rather difficult to find work. And it's rather galling when a chap like Edgar comes along rubbing our noses in his success."

The stories were all similar: Edgar Simmons, the aging actor, suddenly flush with cash and full of himself. But nobody had anything more to say than that. Luckily, Flint had managed to turn up an address—the boarding house where Simmons had last stayed. When he had exhausted his sources (and his liver) in the various actor's bars in the West End, Spector headed there.

The landlady had red hair—blood red, redder than hair has ever been before or since. And her face was uncannily white. She put Spector in mind of accounts he had read of Queen Elizabeth I—more powder and wig than flesh on those old bones. She had a musical, Hebridean accent he could have listened to all day, but she was evidently eager to get down to business and to get this musty old man out of her lovely home.

"Simmons?" she said, "Don't speak that name in front of me."

"So he wasn't a model tenant, then?"

"As a tenant, Mr. Spector, he was no trouble at all. Always quiet and tidy. But what *did* irk me is when he packed up and left without settling his rent."

"When was this?"

"Saturday. I've not seen or heard from him since."

"And he's never done anything like that before?"

"Never. Not once. But there you are, people show you their true colours, don't they?"

Spector had an image in his mind of a shadowed figure standing in the doorway of the Dollis Hill house: a man in a long coat, with a hat brim pulled down over his brow and a scarf pulled up over his mouth. The doctor's visitor, who had so disturbed Olive Turner, and whose presence on the periphery of the investigation was a constant frustration. Could it have been Edgar Simmons?

Flint detested days like this. All that work, and nothing to show for it. No new information, no leads.

That changed at nearly seven p.m. Flint was about to head home for the day when the telephone on his desk began to ring.

Apprehensively he gripped the receiver. "Flint speaking."

"Mr Flint, I need your help." The voice belonged to Floyd Stenhouse, and it sounded as if there were something dreadfully wrong with him. "Can you get over here right away?"

"Why? What's happened?"

"There's somebody after me."

"Who?"

"I don't know. I've never seen him before in my life, but he's after me, I can tell you that much. I was at the studio, you see. But he followed me back here. And now I think he's in the building."

Flint snapped his fingers, gesticulating at the blank sheaf of paper in front of him, and a desk sergeant duly supplied him with a pencil. "Where are you now?"

"I'm at home in my apartment. Dufresne Court. He's in the building. I know he's in the building, Mr. Flint. Get here as soon as you can."

"Stay there. Don't go anywhere. I'm on my way," said Flint, before hanging up the phone.

Hook was nowhere to be found. A brief recce in the squad room rustled up two of the sturdiest-looking uniformed officers the division had to offer: Constables Bream and Harrow. Men of good standing, not to mention intimidating physical stature. Flint enlisted them for the trip over to Dufresne Court.

They travelled by car. It was a tight squeeze, but Flint still found the room to tap out a squib of tobacco into his pipe and ignite it.

They arrived at the immense art deco edifice within ten minutes. Flint led the way imperiously through to the foyer. The desk clerk, Royce, looked up from his crossword.

"Can I help you gentlemen?"

"We're here to see Floyd Stenhouse. Police business."

They strode toward the elevator, but Flint saw from the row of bulbs above the metal cage that it was up on the fourth floor. "No time," he said, heading for the staircase. "Four floors. Eight flights. I hope we're feeling fit this evening, gentlemen?" And with that, he began bounding up the steps, two at a time. When they reached the fourth floor—Flint barely breaking a sweat—the inspector led them along to Floyd Stenhouse's place. He pressed the doorbell. When the door was not immediately answered, he hammered on it with a heavy fist. Still no answer. He cast a sideways glance at the two constables and was about to knock again when a soft sound emerged, like an intake of breath from behind the door: "Who's there?" A quavering voice.

"It's Flint."

Various bolts and chains were unclasped on the other side of the door. There issued the final click of a key turning in a lock and Floyd Stenhouse, looking sweaty and emaciated, admitted them to the apartment. When they were inside, the musician peeped out into the corridor, checking they had arrived unaccompanied. Then he slammed shut the door and pressed his back up against it, as though against some invading force.

"Now," said Flint, "what's this all about?"

"I know how this may appear to you. But I'm *not* paranoid, Mr Flint. Believe me, I'm not. He's here somewhere. In the building. He wants to kill me."

Flint puffed on his pipe and said: "Why don't we go and sit down, and you can tell me the whole thing from the beginning."

When they were all installed in sinking armchairs—the constables looking distinctly ill at ease, with their kneecaps around their ears—Floyd Stenhouse began to tell his story. "I saw him when I was coming out of the studio in Goodge Street. At first I thought nothing of it." He poured himself a brandy with a tremulous hand, sloshing a dab of the amber fluid onto the wooden countertop. "Something to drink, gentlemen?"

"No," Flint answered before either of the uniforms could open their mouths. "Go on with your story."

"I'd never seen him before in my life. He was dressed in a long black coat and a trilby hat with downturned brim. He looked as though he was almost trying to hide his face, somehow. As though he knew I'd recognise him, or remember him. He had a scarf bundled up around his neck, you see, and it all but covered his mouth."

"So you couldn't make out his facial features? Then how can you be sure you hadn't seen him before?"

Stenhouse moistened his lips before taking another gulp of brandy. "I know there's a perception of me as some kind of a misanthrope, and perhaps I am. I know very few people in London, and those I do are close friends, people who would *never* play a trick like that on me. Anyway, I thought little of it at first. But then I spotted him on the omnibus which took me to Charing Cross. And finally, when I arrived back here, I saw him crossing the road behind me as I ducked inside."

"Harrow," Flint turned to one of the uniformed officers, "let's go back downstairs and talk to the chap on the desk. See if he saw anybody lurking around. And we must try and get hold of that lift boy."

"Pete?" said Stenhouse. "What about him?"

"We didn't see him when we arrived."

"I don't trust that boy," Stenhouse continued between glugs of brandy.

"Now I need you to answer this question very carefully, Mr. Stenhouse. Can you think of any reason why somebody might *want* to follow you back here?"

"It was a threat, Mr. Flint. He must . . . I don't know, he must think I know something."

"About what?"

"Why, the murder, of course."

"Now let me get this straight," Flint announced, peering out the window and down at the cobbled courtyard below. "You seem to be assuming that this man who followed you home is the same man who called at Dollis Hill the night Rees was murdered."

"Well, who else could it be?"

"I can think of plenty of people. I'd have thought it could realistically have been *anybody*. What was it about him that convinced you he was something to do with the murder?"

"There was a look about him, Mr. Flint. A look deep in his eyes."

Flint turned to the other uniformed officer. "Bream, I want you to stay here. Don't leave Mr. Stenhouse alone for a *second*, understand? Harrow and I are going to question the desk clerk, then we're going to search this building from top to bottom. See what we can rustle up."

Flint headed out into the empty corridor and then along toward the elevator. His footsteps echoed hollowly on the tiles. In spite of himself and everything he had faced in his years at the Yard, he felt a tingle of fear creeping down the back of his neck. A prickling at the base of his hairline. He wished he had a revolver in his hand.

The elevator was empty. Where was the boy? That was the first mystery. Flint and Harrow stepped inside, and Flint himself jabbed the button for the ground floor.

In the foyer, the two men returned to the clerk's desk. "Have you seen anybody suspicious come into the building?"

Royce was startled. "Why, no. Apart from yourselves, no one's been in since Mr. Stenhouse himself arrived back here an hour ago."

"And was he followed?"

"I'm sure I wouldn't know anything about that."

Flint grunted. "And what about Pete Hobbs, the lift boy?"

"Most likely enjoying a cigarette break, sir. Such 'breaks' have been known to last over an hour, sir. My superiors have been informed."

"He wasn't here when we arrived."

"As I say, sir, his lack of attentiveness has been well noted. I can only apologise."

"Never mind the apology, where *is* he? The elevator was up on the fourth floor with nobody in it."

Royce was intractable. "I can only apologise. Perhaps he's in the yard to the rear of the building? I would accompany you myself, sir, but I'm afraid *I* am not permitted to leave my post."

Flint and the constable headed for the doorway Royce had indicated, which led through a kitchen and washroom and out onto the square cobbled courtyard. The evening air was threaded with chill, and Flint almost shuddered as he stepped outside. Pete Hobbs was nowhere about.

"Stay here," Flint said to Constable Harrow. Then he stepped softly across the yard. His gaze had been caught by a narrow alleyway opposite, which no doubt led through to the street on the other side. As he approached the alley, he became conscious of the silence. It swallowed him like a cocoon. The air was still. The few lights in the windows behind him cast languid shadows across the courtyard. But the alleyway was in darkness.

"Pete!" Flint called out. "Pete Hobbs! Are you there?"

A shadow—a quick black shape—scuttled into his eyeline. "Pete! Is that you?"

The shape stood and did not move. Flint felt the scorch of angry, invisible eyes on him. "Who is that? Who's there?"

He realised for the first time how vulnerable he had let himself become. He could neither see nor identify this man in the shadows. He had no weapon, not even a torch.

The man—for it could only be a man—stood motionless in the mouth of the alleyway. There were no discernible features—not even his coat and hat. Flint pressed on into the darkness.

That was when the shot came.

There is often talk of a shot "ringing out," but in this case it was a truism. The sound was so shattering, so fearfully reverberant, that it seemed to bounce round the yard in a hellish echo. Flint flung himself face-first at the ground, but the bullet went wide. While the shot was still fading, there followed the sound of running footsteps, retreating along the alleyway.

Suddenly, Harrow was there helping him to his feet. Flint was panting, unable to fully reconcile how close he had come to death. "He—he went down the alley. Get after him, Harrow. But be careful, for God's sake! He's armed." Harrow thundered along the alley after the vanished shadow-man.

Flint limped toward the mouth of the alleyway. The street lamp at its far end gave the stretch of ground a lambent glow. He could make out only dustbins and empty crates. But as he proceeded, his foot brushed something. He knelt down to examine it by matchlight. In the sudden flare of that little orange flame, he saw that it was a revolver. A thin stream of smoke twisted from the barrel.

"Who was it?" said a low, hoarse voice, choked by terror.

Flint whirled round and, in the glow of the match he made out the face of Della Cookson.

"Who fired the shot?" she said, her brow creased and her mouth slackly open. She looked utterly dumbstruck. Not an image she would like the scandal rags to print.

"Miss Cookson," Flint breathed. "And just what brings *you* here?"

<hr />

While Flint and Harrow commenced their search of Dufresne Court, Constable Bream stayed behind with Floyd Stenhouse in apartment 408. He had been offered a cigarette by his host, which he accepted gratefully. But it was not yet lit when the doorbell rang. Stenhouse, who was trying vainly to strike a match, jolted as though with electricity.

"What is it? Who's that?"

"Nothing to fret about, sir," said Bream, removing the unlit cigarette from his mouth and slipping it into his pocket for later. "It'll be the inspector, that's who."

"Just be careful, man. That's all I'm saying."

Constable Bream strode toward the door. But the nearer he got, the slower his pace. He found the uncanny atmosphere of the place was getting to him. He wondered who was *really* waiting for him on the other side of that door.

His hand hovered over the doorknob.

"Inspector?" he called out. But there was no answer.

With a breath, he flung open the door.

Bream found himself confronted by an empty corridor. Stepping out of the apartment, he looked up and down and found the whole place deserted.

"Who is it?" came Stenhouse's tremulous voice from behind him.

"There's nobody here," he answered, bemused.

"What?" Now Stenhouse appeared at his shoulder, peering up and down the corridor. It was then that they heard the shot.

"What was *that*?" Stenhouse shrieked. This was all getting undignified. The musician was obviously an hysteric.

"A shot, sir. Somewhere down below. I'd better go."

"Then I'm coming with you."

"Sir, I'd advise against that."

"Oh, you'd rather I stay here on my own? God knows how many there are. It might be a whole army out there."

"Well," Bream said, shrugging, "it's your funeral, Mr. Stenhouse."

The two men headed out into the corridor, Bream aiming for the stairs.

"Where are you going?" said Stenhouse.

"I'm walking down."

"Why not take the elevator?"

"Trust me, sir. In these circumstances it's better to be out in the open than cooped up in a metal box."

When they got to the ground floor, Bream led the way out into the foyer. Royce looked to be quivering behind his desk.

"What is it?" he yelped. "What's happening? I'd look for myself but I'm afraid I'm not permitted . . ."

"Nothing to fret about," Bream lied gamely, "everything's under control."

He headed for the courtyard with Floyd Stenhouse skulking behind him. But he was met halfway by a breathless Inspector Flint, accompanied—bizarrely enough—by Della Cookson. "What the hell are you two doing here?" the inspector demanded. "Why aren't you upstairs? I told you to stay in the apartment."

"I-I thought I'd come and see if I could assist, sir," Bream stammered.

"And bring Stenhouse with you? My God, man, use your nut. There's nothing you can do anyway. There was a gunman, but he's gone. Harrow went running after him, but couldn't keep up. The bastard caught us completely unawares."

"Where's Harrow now?"

"Still out there. There's evidence to be collected. But come on, let's get Mr. Stenhouse back upstairs. I have one or two questions for you as well, Miss Cookson."

They headed back to the foyer, where the desk clerk was still panicking. "What is it? What's going on?" he cried.

"Just a little skirmish out in the courtyard. It's all over now, I can assure you."

They huddled around the desk and tried to unpick what had just happened. Who fired the shot? And who was the target? Soon, Constable Harrow returned, still breathless.

Flint turned his attention to Della. "You'd better tell us what you're doing here, Miss Cookson. And no lies, please."

She gave a sigh. "No way out of it this time, is there? I was visiting you, Floyd."

"Mr. Stenhouse here? And why would you be doing that?"

She gave a sly smile. Floyd blinked away his embarrassment, and could not quite meet anyone's gaze.

"I wasn't aware there was a law against it. But as I think you know, he and I are old acquaintances. We still correspond from time to time. Isn't that so, Floyd?"

"It's true, Inspector," Stenhouse volunteered. "We were childhood friends."

Flint tapped his notebook with the nib of his pencil. He looked at Della. "I don't believe you've answered my question."

"I came here to ask Floyd a favour, a personal favour. And it's of no relevance to you, so I don't see why I should tell."

"I think you'll agree this is something of a sticky situation for you, Miss. It's the second time you've arrived on the scene of a crime without a decent explanation as to what you were doing there. I think I'd be forgiven for drawing an uneasy correlation between the events."

"Look," she snapped, "if you have to know—I mean *really* have to know—I came to see Floyd because I need to borrow some money."

Flint was momentarily flummoxed. He suddenly became aware of Royce the desk clerk, earwigging unobtrusively. "Shall we continue this discussion upstairs?" he said.

They made for the elevator: Flint, Della, Stenhouse, and the two breathless constables. It would be a tight squeeze, but they would just about manage it. And it was better than any more of that splitting-up nonsense. The automatic doors slithered open. Flint froze.

At his feet lay what first appeared to be a heap of sackcloth, sprawled on the elevator floor. It was only when he stepped closer that he realised he was looking at the foetally curled form of Pete Hobbs.

"Stand back," he said to the others. He and the constables piled in to get a better look. Della covered her mouth with her hand and turned away from the sight in horror. Flint leaned in over the boy and held a palm up to his face, just below the nostrils, but there issued no discernible breath.

"He's dead," said Flint. "Looks to have been strangled."

Coiled about the throat of the unfortunate elevator boy was a length of rope. It had bitten into his neck so hard it drew blood. This was the work of an almost unholy strength.

"But what I don't understand," Flint continued to no one in particular, "is how did he get in here?" He called out to Royce, who still refused to leave the front desk: "Did the elevator move at all since Harrow and I stepped out of it?"

"No, sir."

"Well, how did the corpse get *in* here then? Did you see Pete Hobbs at all? Could someone have carried him into the lift while it was on the ground floor?"

"No, sir. I had my eye on the elevator doors the entire time. I would have seen if anyone had so much as gone near them. And I can promise you for definite that no one did."

Flint looked up at the elevator ceiling, the width and breadth of which was taken up by a large square maintenance trapdoor. But this was bolted shut on the inside. "So," Flint concluded quietly, "another impossibility."

The ambulance was duly called, along with the crime scene photographer and various uniforms to patrol the perimeter and gather statements. But Flint knew they would find nothing. He had been on the scene himself the entire time, at the very moment the murder was committed. And he had seen absolutely nothing.

Flint himself supervised the search of Dufresne Court from top to bottom, but the fifth floor was indeed unoccupied. The flats were empty and bare and showed no sign of habitation. As they worked downward, the residents were woken and questioned, but nobody had heard anything save for that pesky gunshot, which many had mistaken for a car backfiring. All the windows were locked up tight, and there was no evidence anywhere of a break-in.

The pathologist who examined Pete Hobbs offered little in the way of insight. "I can tell you he was killed in the last hour. Very fresh. Strangled. Garrotted, more like."

"Can you get anything from the rope?"

"I'll know more when I can have a look at it in isolation. But for now I'll say, unlikely. It's just an ordinary length of rope. You might find it in a factory, or a warehouse, or a dockyard, or anywhere things are tied."

"But you're absolutely certain he was killed within the last hour?"

"Positive."

"Then that rules out Stenhouse," Flint murmured. "He was with us the whole time. But it doesn't rule out Della. She was in the courtyard when the shot was fired, but she might have killed the boy beforehand."

"All due respect," said the pathologist, "I don't believe this is a woman's crime."

Flint ignored this. "Have you any idea how the killer might have infiltrated the lift itself?"

"That's your department, not mine. But are you absolutely positive of the desk clerk's honesty?"

"I don't need to be. I was down here most of the time myself. And I don't see how Hobbs could have got into the lift. It didn't move up from the ground floor from the moment I myself stepped out of it with Constable Harrow, and nobody went in or out while it was on the ground floor."

Constable Bream nodded. "That'd mean he died while all that business in the courtyard was happening."

"I see now," Flint continued. "It was all a smokescreen. A distraction. He wanted to split us up. And it worked. It does raise a question, though, as to *why* the elevator boy had to die."

"He must have known something or seen something."

"But," supplied the constable, "the desk clerk had a perfect view of the elevator doors at all times. He's convinced nobody went in or out of the elevator itself while it was on the ground floor during those few minutes."

"And we were all together from the time of the gunshot."

"Then maybe," the pathologist posited with undue flippancy, "you should get your magic friend to help you. This seems more his forte than mine."

Flint strode off without another word.

A cadre of reporters had gathered on the steps of the building. Their lenses flared and photobulbs shattered as Flint stepped outside. Amid the babble, he made out snippets of questions: "Is it another impossible crime, sir?"

"Still no ideas whodunit?"

". . . the same man?"

". . . it happened in an elevator, is that true, Inspector?"

"What's it going to take to stop the phantom killer, sir?"

Flint didn't speak. He stood at the top of the steps as the photographers jostled for prime position, and quietly filled his pipe. He ignited it and breathed in a warm plume of tobacco smoke. Then, with an air of resolution, he marched away. The photographers watched him go. It was close to dawn.

Wednesday, September 16, 1936

XIII

THE MADMAN, ESPINA

Flint felt a sense of déjà vu as he stepped across the threshold of the Black Pig in Putney. Joseph Spector was in his customary seat in the snug, this time with a deck of tarot cards spread out in front of him. It was now the morning of the sixteenth, but the dust of last night's debacle had not yet settled.

"Care for a reading?" the old man asked.

"Have you heard?"

"About the elevator boy? I'm afraid I have. Bad news travels fast."

"And what do you make of it?"

"Very little, thus far. But there is *one* thing I know."

"And what's that?"

"You remember Royce, the desk clerk?"

"Remember him? I've been interrogating him these last eight hours."

"Well, it turns out my bestowing a business card on him was a worthwhile investment. He telephoned me this morning. It seems he's a little too frightened of you, Inspector, to give you the whole truth. But he wanted to tell *somebody* what he knew."

"And what's that?"

"The name of the man who ran away from you in the alley."

"Oh yes?" Flint was evidently sceptical. "Well, fire away."

"Better if I show you," said Spector, before calling out: "Bill, could you come in here, please?"

And an old man entered the snug. This fellow was a poor, flea-bitten mendicant, dissolute and dirt caked. But there was intelligence in his sunken, red-rimmed eyes, and pain was etched in the creases of his face. He wore his left arm in a sling.

"Who's this?" demanded Flint.

"Allow me to present Bill Harper," said Spector.

Flint, his weary, half-lidded eyes unblinking, persisted: "And who's Bill Harper when he's at home?"

"Aha. That's just it. Poor Bill no longer *has* a home. And that's why he was in the alley last night. You might notice poor Bill has suffered a mishap. He was shot by an unidentified gunman. But perhaps you would like to tell the story, Bill?"

The old man eased himself into a seat, wincing as the sling round his arm brushed the edge of the table. "I've been sleeping rough for a while, ever since I got laid off at the factory. Nights are getting colder now, and it's hard to find somewhere decent to lay your head. So I've been kipping round the back of the flats."

Flint leaned forward on his elbows, his interest piqued. "In the alley behind Dufresne Court?"

"That's it. That fellow Royce isn't so bad, you know. He's been sneaking me food now and then, little things like that. Anyway, I was there last night when the shooting started."

"Did you see anybody?"

"Only yourself, sir. And the lady. I was asleep when your shouting woke me up. So I got up to see what was going on, and that's when the bugger shot me."

"The bullet from the revolver grazed his arm," Spector explained. "And quite naturally for someone who has just been shot, Bill was quick to make his escape."

Flint groaned. "So you're telling me that *you* were the man I saw running out of the alley?"

Bill nodded glumly. "Doctors tell me it's not too serious—at least, it could have been worse."

"And did you see who fired the shot?"

"No. I was stowed in the alley when I felt a sting, like a bee. Then a split second later I heard the shot. And I got scared, sir. So I ran."

"And where did you go?"

"Hospital, sir. I was bleeding badly."

Flint's manner softened a little. "I trust the doctors treated you kindly?"

"Most agreeable they were, sir."

"But you've no inkling who pulled the trigger."

The beggar shook his head.

"As far as Mr. Harper is concerned," Spector supplied, "the only people in that courtyard were yourself and Della Cookson."

"But that's no use. *Somebody* fired that shot."

"They certainly did. But whoever it was, it certainly wasn't Bill here. Nor was it anybody who went through the alley."

"Well where does that leave us?"

Spector sighed and turned to Bill. He handed him a pound note. "Go and get yourself something to eat, old chum," he said. The old man slipped away as swiftly as he had appeared. Just another of Spector's magic tricks. Then Spector turned his attention to Flint. "Mapping out a sequence of events like those you experienced last night is quite a task. They're all so diffuse and subjective. They rely on the interpretations of the individuals concerned. But for you, Inspector Flint, I'll give it a try."

With a fresh sheaf of notepaper and a pen brimming with ink, the old man began sketching out a timeline for the events.

Flint and his cohort had arrived at Dufresne Court at seven thirty the previous evening. Between eight p.m. and nine, Pete Hobbs was murdered and his body dumped in the elevator. But the elevator did not stop anywhere between the ground floor and the fourth floor, nor did it travel any *higher* than the fourth floor. The fifth floor was unoccupied anyway. With the scene set, Spector turned to the incident itself.

"So what do we know about the gunman in the courtyard?"

"Nothing."

"Do we know what he was shooting at?"

"Not yet. But most likely it was me."

"Why would he do that? Surely it would be better simply to have run? Taking that shot and missing was an unnecessary risk."

"What do *you* think, then?"

Spector did not answer. "Do we know why Della Cookson was there?"

"She *claims* she was after a loan from Stenhouse."

Spector arched an eyebrow. "From Stenhouse?" He considered this. "Perhaps I'd better talk to her again?"

"If you like. If you think it'll get you anywhere. But it couldn't be Della who pulled the trigger. Remember the fingerprints. Della wasn't wearing gloves that night, so by rights her fingerprints would have been all over the revolver if she was the one who did the shooting."

"Unless . . ." Spector added thoughtfully, "there was some trickery. There is *one* way Della might have fired the shot. It would require the use of *two* revolvers. She could have donned a pair of gloves, fired the revolver a moment earlier using something to suppress the sound (a pillow, for instance), then deposited the weapon on the ground waiting to be discovered. Then she could have removed her gloves, taken out a second revolver, and fired that into the air—nice and loud—before returning it to her handbag. Then, when you stepped outside and found the smoking revolver you naturally assumed it was *that* one which had just been fired. And the absence of fingerprints would seem to exonerate Della."

"You don't honestly expect me to buy that nonsense, do you? Of course I searched her bag and there was no second revolver."

Spector's smile was genuine. "Then she could have disposed of it elsewhere. No, Inspector. I'm not expecting you to buy that nonsense. All the same, my hobby is explaining the inexplicable."

"Try as I might, God help me, I still can't pin down just where Miss Della Cookson fits into this business at all."

"No. Just another thread on this particularly tangled web. Incidentally, I've been reading up on kleptomania," Spector said. "It really is a fascinating topic. Typically, it's a symptom rather than a cause, you know. 'Comorbid traumas' are said to be the real root. What we usually find with the kleptomaniac is not at all the archetypal delight in thievery. Quite the opposite. Rather, the thief is plagued by his urges; it is an almost physical compulsion. When confronted by an object he simply has to have it. But he will also be tormented by guilt. Often he'll rely on drug use as a crutch. The patient might as well be possessed by demons. It is a compulsion beyond his control, a build-up of pressure in the brain. And it can *only* be assuaged by stealing.

"A few misconceptions: the kleptomaniac *doesn't* steal for personal gain. He steals simply because he cannot *not* steal. Also, he doesn't steal out of enmity or rancour. The theft is scarcely a conscious act, and the only emotion attached to it is crippling guilt. Usually the object of theft will be some useless item. It is, in fact, quite rare for anything truly valuable to be taken. The monetary worth of the object is of no consideration whatsoever."

After this little lecture, Spector studied Flint, as though trying to gauge the inspector's comprehension of his argument. Then he went on:

"During my travels some years ago I happened to visit the museum at Ghent, in Belgium. They have there a remarkable sequence of portraits by Théodore Géricault. Over a hundred years old, but still so insightful. And beautiful. Géricault's intention was to create a sequence portraying clinical models for a variety of diseases of the mind. He painted ten patients at the Salpêtrière asylum, and somehow he managed to convey the very soul of each unfortunate individual. Quite an achievement. But there's one painting in particular, *Portrait of a Kleptomaniac*, which has been haunting me lately. That rigid, intractable face. A tortured dullness to the eyes. He is looking at nothing. And yet there is such torment there. Gericault was one of the first to portray the mentally sick as *human beings*, like you or me. He saw past the behavioural traits to the fragility, the delicacy. The humanity. I think about that portrait a lot."

"And do you see that same 'tortured dullness' in Della Cookson's eyes?" Flint asked.

Spector considered the question. "What I see when I look in Della's eyes is something altogether different. Something darker. It makes me wonder what torments she has endured in her life. Can we believe she took *El Nacimiento*? Instinct would tell us not. The description in Dr. Rees's notes is of an opportunity thief, one who steals because she *can*. Nick-nacks, small objects of little value. It's the object itself, feeling the weight of it in her hand. Certainly *not* material value or anything so crude. *El Nacimiento* is not the kind of object our actress would typically favour. Too large, bulky, and cumbersome. And as we know, its worth is of little consequence to her."

"I don't think you can make these sweeping statements about her character. Even Rees struggled to pin down what motivates her. Remember the watch? She had a prime opportunity to pinch Marcus Bowman's watch but she *didn't*. It's not for us to say whether something would or would not appeal to her wretched brain."

"Point taken," Spector acceded, "but that still leaves us with the question of opportunity. As far as we know, everything she took, she took because it was *there*. But *El Nacimiento* was not 'there' in any way that would be meaningful to Della. It was under lock and key, in a trunk under Teasel's bed. Out of her grasp. She doesn't crack safes or pick locks. She has always been more of a pickpocket than a master thief.

"Think carefully," he suddenly demanded, turning on Flint. "The answer is in the doctor's notes. Think about that encounter she had with Marcus Bowman. Aside from the watch business, what interested *me* is the doctor's account of what Bowman himself said during the encounter. According to the notes, Bowman recognised Della instantly. But when I attended the opening night of *Miss Death*, I distinctly recall overhearing Bowman and Lidia in an awkward little exchange where Bowman pretended not to know who Della was. He even referred to her as 'Helen' Cookson. Which proves nothing in itself, but it raises questions. Why did Marcus Bowman pretend he'd never met Della before? And why in front of Lidia, of all people?"

Flint drummed the tabletop with his fingers. "So Bowman *did* know Della. And in his ham-fisted way, he was trying to stop Lidia from finding out."

Spector nodded. "Let's pursue this train of thought further. Bowman put on a show of recognising Della at Dollis Hill. And then he put on a show of *not* recognising her at the Pomegranate. And Della didn't take the watch. The only reason she wouldn't have seized that opportunity is that she recognised Bowman too, and she was startled. Scared, even. She hadn't expected to see him there. And she did not *want* to see him there. But why? It's not too much of a step to conclude that they were in some kind of clandestine relationship. One of life's embarrassing coincidences: she was having an affair with her psychiatrist's prospective son-in-law. Not as unlikely as it seems at first glance. Bowman is especially adept at inveigling invites to high society events. And Della, as an actress, is always a focal point at such events. With circumstances like these, it would have been unlikely for them *not* to have met before.

"And here's something else: Benjamin Teasel was very taken with Della's reaction to the painting when he showed it to her at the party. He seemed to feel there was something 'uncanny' about the way she looked at the canvas. What does he mean by that, do you think?"

"Well," said Flint, "there's only one way to find out. We'll go and see Della again. I'll get to the bottom of this if it kills me. But please, Spector, do me one favour first. Buy me a beer, eh?"

They found Della alone in her dressing room in the Pomegranate. Her hand quivered slightly as she applied her makeup.

"You're going ahead with the performance?" said Flint.

"I know you'll think me callous. And I don't care. I need to make a living, and thanks to last night's shenanigans, I did *not* manage to get hold of my loan from Floyd Stenhouse."

"You never did answer my question last night, Miss Cookson—what did you want the money for? Is it blackmail?"

"If it is," she said, straightening her corset, "then it's none of your business."

"Mr. Flint, if I may . . ." Spector interjected, "I have just one question for you, Della."

She turned away from the mirror to look at him and there was a quiet anxiety in her eyes. "You may as well ask, Joseph."

"It's not about Floyd Stenhouse. Or Pete Hobbs. Or even Dr. Rees. It's about *El Nacimiento.*"

"What about it?"

"To your knowledge, did Benjamin Teasel show the painting to anyone else the night of the party?"

"No. He didn't. And I know that for a fact because he told me so. He said I was the only one on whom he was 'bestowing this gift.'"

"And when he showed you the painting, the room was dark?"

"It was moonlit. I could only see by the light from that small window. He didn't turn on the lamps because he said the work was best viewed by natural light, such as it was."

"But you were alone?"

"Quite alone. At least—" She stopped herself.

"What is it?"

"No, it's nothing. Probably nothing."

Flint might have liked to push this further, but Spector was content to let it lie.

"Do you know anything about the mad Spaniard, Manolito Espina?"

"Only that he was a painter."

"I think you're being modest. I think you know more about him than that. But maybe you *don't* know that one of the symptoms of his so-called madness was his absolute conviction that his paintings were predictions of the future. His warped *Landscapes of Lower Hell* sequence was all the more startling when it was first unveiled because Espina accompanied it with the caveat that it was a painting from life. He was lucky they didn't burn him at the stake."

Della's voice was flat. "What's your point, Joseph?"

"Only that verisimilitude in art can have a strange effect on its audience. There's no denying that *El Nacimiento* is a work of startling genius. But I've been trying to work out why it affected you in the way that it did." There followed a brief pause. "What is the subject of the painting?" Spector inquired idly.

"Does it matter?"

Spector blinked.

"Mother and child," Della sighed.

"This is pure supposition," Spector began. "And in a court of law it would be slander. But you won't sue, will you, Della? If we enjoin all the little details, and a few big ones, there is a distinct conclusion to be reached. You and Marcus Bowman had been having an affair. This must have been a source of some considerable emotional torment for you. But the sight of a Renaissance masterpiece depicting a mother and new-born child induced in you a visceral reaction—it sent you running from the party and straight across London to your psychiatrist."

Della smiled mirthlessly, and spoke in waspish tones. "I think you're being oblique about it, but you've known all along, haven't you? Didn't you wonder why I was missing so many rehearsals? Doctor's appointments. Not just Rees; I have a man in Harley Street. And when I began to notice certain . . . changes, I went to him to get myself checked out."

"And?"

She sniffed haughtily. "Not that it's any of your business, Joseph . . . and God forbid you breathe a word of this to anyone . . . but yes. It turns out I'm two months along."

Spector nodded respectfully. "And the father?"

"What about him?"

"Does he know?"

"No he doesn't. What would be the point?"

"It *is* Marcus Bowman, isn't it?"

"Yes, it's Marcus. Of course I didn't know he was engaged to Rees's daughter. That's just an unhappy coincidence. But I honestly couldn't tell you if it would have made a difference or not, even if I had known."

Spector nodded thoughtfully. "What are you going to do?"

"I've been trying to forget about it. Pretend it isn't happening. But there's no escaping it, is there? It'll be painfully obvious to everyone soon enough."

"And you've started drinking again."

"I didn't know what else to do." She was close to tears. "There was no one I could talk to. No one except Dr. Rees, and he was pretty cagy about the whole thing. I told him about it after the show on opening night. He came to my dressing room. And he never said it in so many words, but I couldn't escape the feeling that he disapproved. So I tried to push it from my mind. To focus on the play. That just made things worse. And then, when Teasel showed me that painting . . ." Her eyes overflowed and the tears sluiced down her face.

"My dear," said Spector, patting her arm, "I can only imagine."

"It was like a . . . a shard of ice in my chest. I felt I might die there of shame and fear. What a headline that would have been!" She gave a husky laugh. "I got out of that house as soon as I could. I left the party. And I headed for the only place I could think to go."

"Rees's house."

"Right. The taxi took me straight there. It was maybe fifteen minutes between my leaving Teasel's party and my arriving in Dollis Hill."

Through all of this, Spector's expression had remained intractable. "Benjamin is quite convinced you took the painting."

"I would never do that, Joseph. You must believe me. I know you're aware of my . . . particular affliction"—she could not make eye contact with him when she said it—"but I could never steal something so . . . beautiful. So perfect. It made my heart hurt to look at it."

"All the same, you have to admit the coincidence is unfortunate."

"Oh, the worst. And just my damned luck. Of course I'm going to have to pull out of the production anyway, once *this*" —she looked down at her stomach—"gets too cumbersome to hide. But I had hoped not to go under a cloud of scandal. Now it looks like that's unavoidable."

"Not necessarily. After all, the maids and just about everyone else at the party can confirm that when you left you were not carrying a large painting in a wooden frame. Can you think of anyone else at the party that night who *might* have known where Teasel kept *El Nacimiento*?"

She shook her head. "Teasel and I were the only ones up there. I mean, I can't prove it, but I know we were the only ones in that room when he opened the chest."

"And everyone else at the party seems able to alibi each other. The only explanation would be if someone else—an outsider—got into the house unnoticed." Spector had begun to pick up speed, as though he were on the verge of some great revelation. "Now we've been told by the maids on duty that it would be impossible. We've taken them at their word, because they were in a position to monitor the comings and goings of all the guests."

"Where are you going with this, Spector?" Flint demanded.

"A curious thought . . . do you remember the Chesterton story 'The Invisible Man'? In it, a seemingly phantom killer manages to escape the scene of his crime undetected. Nobody is seen entering or leaving the house in question."

"So? How did the fellow manage it?"

"The problem is really one of semantics, and what we mean by 'invisible.' Invisible as in "cannot be seen by the naked eye," or invisible as in "not *perceived* by the naked eye." The maids were told there'd been a burglary, and so when you quizzed them about whether they had seen anything suspicious, any uninvited guests or such like, they naturally pictured a 'burglar.' That is, a man, well built and gruff looking. Something uneasy about him. They used their imaginations. But because they had not encountered anybody who matched that description, they were happy to confirm there had been no unexpected guest at all."

"I see," said Flint. "So you reckon the thief was someone who fitted in. Someone who wasn't necessarily a guest, but who *looked* as though they might have been."

"Quite. Someone in evening wear. Someone female. In the eyes of those maids, someone like that could not possibly be up to no good. So, consciously or otherwise, they excluded her from the accounts they gave the police."

"But Joseph," said Della, "you need to think about this: whoever took the painting had to get the keys from around Teasel's neck. That's why he's so fixed on me. Because I was tipsy and I gave him a kiss before I left the party."

"I remember. But then, the party was a rather intimate occasion. We were all crammed in quite close together in that house. Anybody could have lifted it."

"Without him noticing? Possibly. But then, surely he would have noticed if it was somebody he hadn't invited?"

"Not necessarily. After all, it was a booze-sodden affair. But there's one thing which I believe I can say for sure. If it had been a *man* who did it, Benjamin would have known. But I think a *woman* could quite easily have snaked her arms around his neck—perhaps during a dance—and snagged the keys without him realising."

"You think it was someone he danced with? Danced with her, but didn't recognise her? That would mean it must have happened later that night, when everyone was too drunk to care what was going on."

"Benjamin was so adamant that you, Della, were the only one who could have taken the keys from around his neck. But now I think I can see why. He was so *desperate* for it to be you because he's been looking for an excuse to oust you from the production. It would be most convenient for him if you turned out to be an art thief into the bargain."

"But I'm not! You believe that, don't you, Joseph?"

"I do," he answered, placing a hand over hers. "I wholeheartedly believe you did not steal that painting. And I think we may finally be closer to finding out who did."

"Who, then? Do you have an idea?"

"Well, let's weigh our options. It was a woman, because a woman would have been able to drape her arms around

Benjamin's neck in such a nonchalant manner as to extract the keys. We believe it happened later in the evening—after you had left, in other words—because Benjamin would have been less likely to notice it happening with a few drinks in him. If it was somebody on the guest list (which we have effectively disproven, because they were all searched and yet nothing was found) then they could have done the deed at any time in the night. But if we're operating under the assumption that it was an outsider, then this enables us to narrow down the stretch of time in which they may have entered the house.

"You left at eleven. Let's say the thief was already in the house at that point, but unnoticed. Someone who blended neatly into the background. Someone who could have crept up the stairs after you and listened at the door as Benjamin showed you the painting."

He trailed off.

Flint pounced. "You've thought of something?"

"I have. Thank you for your time, Della. I'll speak to you again soon."

"What was that all about?" Flint demanded as the two men strode away from the Pomegranate. "All the mystery-man business? I thought you were at least going to *mention* the murder last night at Dufresne Court. And do you know who took the painting, or don't you?"

"Well, let's just say I know who *didn't* take the painting. Della was struck dumb by *El Nacimiento*. The depiction of a mother and newborn child is particularly emotive. It also explains why she dashed from the room, before heading off at the first opportunity to visit her psychiatrist. The enormity of her ordeal was finally becoming clear to her, and she was realising she could not cope. We can piece together Della's motivation from here. It shocked her. It gave her a sudden flood of emotion. It gave her a sense of longing, but also an inner agony. Because she saw in the face of that mother her own face. *This* is why she hastily excused herself and departed from Teasel's party. It's why she rushed across London to the Rees house. He was the only one she could trust with this secret of hers. The only man she could rely on. She needed help. But what did she find, on her arrival at Dollis Hill? A murder scene. It was too late. So naturally she lapsed into silence.

"From there it's simply a matter of connecting the dots. The loan she wanted from Stenhouse was to pay for a certain back-street medical procedure to take care of her problem. But I'm sure that even under pain of death you'll never get her to admit it."

"If that's the case, then you're saying she had nothing to do with the theft, *or* with the killing of Dr. Rees?"

"That's what I'm saying."

"Then who did?"

"Ah. Well. I think I may have a few ideas on that front as well. But this needs to be dealt with sensitively. And sensibly. I need to talk to Marcus Bowman."

They found Bowman at Robinson's, his club in Regent Street. He was playing billiards and swigging scotch. A quick word from the inspector and he accompanied them out into the corridor, so that they might have a quiet word.

"What is it *now*? I have work I could be doing, you know."

"Just one little question for you, Mr Bowman," said Spector with a polite smile. "Please tell me why you lied to us about where you were on the night of the murder?"

Whatever Bowman had anticipated, it was not this. "What the hell are you talking about?"

"We know you and Lidia were *not* together all evening, as you originally claimed. Eyewitness reports tell us you created quite a stir on the dance floor at the Palmyra Club. But you weren't dancing, were you? You argued. A fierce confrontation. Am I wrong? And she left you and stormed out of the club in a state of distress. And you tried to follow her. But she was too quick for you, wasn't she? You lost her somewhere in the London night. So you took a cab back to Dollis Hill, didn't you? And you were alone. Please do stop me if anything I'm saying is incorrect."

Bowman gulped loudly. "It was only a white lie, I swear. I didn't kill the old man, but then neither did she."

"No. But you *did* woefully underestimate her intelligence, didn't you? She saw through your little deceptions instantly. Perhaps she even enjoyed toying with you. Of *course* she knew about Della Cookson. And we know she read her father's notes and discussed them with him in depth. So she understood Della's kleptomania.

"All right. Let's go back to the night of the murder. How did the evening begin? You and Lidia went out to dinner. As far as we can tell, this at least was a civilised affair. But then you left the Savoy and headed for the Palmyra. It's harder to keep track of you from this point onward. But we know you were drinking. And that you argued. Of course we've no way of confirming you were at the Palmyra *all* night."

Flint, feeling a little left out, put in: "They didn't go back to the Rees house . . ."

Spector jabbed the air with a finger: "Right! They didn't. *But* they could easily have gone to Benjamin Teasel's house. It's only a short distance from Soho."

"Why would they do that?"

Spector turned on Flint. "Is it so strange to imagine that Lidia confronted her fiancé about his affair? Of course he denied it, didn't you, Mr. Bowman? But she knew. And so she stormed out. She also knew about Teasel's party, because her father had been invited. So she must have made her way there on foot. The house party was easy to spot on that otherwise quiet, twilit street; the music was loud and the place blazed with lights.

"So she infiltrated the place without difficulty, breezing straight past the maids in all her finery, with her characteristic air of gentility and entitlement. Once inside, she could watch Della from afar. She could follow Teasel and Della up the stairs, perhaps listening at the door or even spying at the keyhole as they looked at *El Nacimiento*. Teasel himself was unable to remember exactly who it was he danced with that night, and who could have snagged the keys. And he thought only Della had been with him for the unveiling. He didn't bank on there being a hidden observer. But it wouldn't take much for *Lidia* to pinch the keys, sneak back upstairs again, and steal *El Nacimiento* from its hiding place."

"But wait a moment," said Flint. "How did she get it out of the house? We've pretty much established there's no way she could have carried it out past the maids."

"Ah. Yes, I'm afraid that's partially my fault. You see, I've been rather fixated on the idea that when the painting was taken, it was still in its frame."

"You mean she cut it from the frame?"

"Precisely. I am not sure what exactly she used, but a small pair of scissors or even a sharpened fingernail might have done it. It's an ugly thought, but I believe that's what happened."

"Then surely the frame should still have been in the room?"

"By rights, yes. But to further confuse matters, she decided to steal that too."

"How?"

"Well, Lidia did not consider the frame to be of any particular value. To her, it was merely an encumbrance. The *painting* was the true object of her plan. So, once the painting was free of its giltwood moorings, I believe she broke the frame into four pieces and fed them out the window one at a time. They would have clattered to the pavement outside, but the jazz music and general sounds of merriment would certainly have masked the noise. Then Lidia simply bolted the window again and, with the furled painting tucked away in her dress, she exited the party as swiftly as she arrived—pausing to retrieve the broken bits of picture frame, of course.

"So then she headed for home, presumably disposing of the frame en route. She must have been very pleased with herself."

Flint paced up and down along the corridor. "It *could* have happened that way. Yes, I suppose it could. Teasel believed that only Della knew the painting was there, so naturally his attention was focused on her. And because every *invited* guest was searched by the police this looked to be an impossible crime, when in fact it was everything but."

"Right!" Spector enthused.

"But that still leaves us with questions. For instance, it would mean Lidia had the painting on her when she arrived back at Dollis Hill. So what did she do with it?"

Turning again on Bowman, Spector demanded: "Lidia stole *El Nacimiento*, didn't she? And you covered it up for her. From the club she went to Teasel's house, didn't she? She was planning to confront Della, to get the whole sordid business out in the open. But when she slipped into the house unnoticed and followed the host and his guest of honour up the stairs, a better scheme presented itself to her. Bearing in mind Della's case history, she decided to pounce on this as an opportunity for a frame-up, if you'll forgive the term. So she took the painting and hid it somewhere. And it's still there, isn't it?"

Marcus blanched. He looked about to collapse. Even his moustache had wilted. When he spoke, it was with perfect crispness and clarity. All his affectations had deserted him. "I took a cab back to Dollis Hill, like you said. If you remember, I had left my car there so Lidia and I could take a cab. I sat in my car and waited for her to come home. I was too scared to go up to the house on my own. Didn't fancy playing the buffoon with the old man. I didn't know where she'd gone, or what she'd done, but I was certain she'd be coming back home eventually, so I thought it would be a safe bet to just sit and wait for her."

"When you met up, you entered the house together. And it was as if you hadn't parted company at all that evening."

Marcus nodded. "I realised something iffy had gone on when all the police cars showed up. At first I thought Lidia might have done something silly. I mean, something violent. Gone for Della with claws out or something. But when we stepped into the house together and I found out what had happened to her father, we didn't need to say a word to each other. Neither of us could, or would, have done something like that. But at the same time, neither of us had a decent alibi. So we did what *anybody* would do in that situation. The only sensible thing. We lied."

"Honestly," said Spector after a pause, "I can't tell you I would have behaved any differently. But this means *you* were in your car outside the Rees house when the murder occurred."

Bowman did not speak for a moment. He was thinking very hard, you could almost hear the cogs whirring in his brain. "I suppose I must have been, yes."

"Then chances are you would have seen the murderer leaving the house."

"Chances do seem quite high, don't they?"

"Well?"

"I may well have seen him. But I couldn't tell you who he is."

"Let me guess—a nondescript man in a hat and coat?"

"A fellow came out the front door at about eleven forty-five. And the other fellow came round the side about a minute later. They both left in the same direction."

"Hold it a moment," said Flint. "We know about the fellow who left by the front door. He's the one who visited Rees. But who was it that came round the side?"

"I couldn't make him out. But there was definitely a man who slipped out the side gate of the house. He must have come from the back garden."

Flint and Spector looked at each other. "I need you to think very carefully before answering, Mr. Bowman," said Flint. "Who was this second man?"

Bowman was shaking his head slowly. "I can't say. I'm sorry. I know you'd like me to. But I just couldn't tell you who he was. He was in the rain, and he had his hat pulled down low."

"But he *definitely* came from the back garden of the Rees place?"

"Yes. Absolutely. He looked to be following the fellow who came out the front door."

Flint and Spector were both thinking the same thought. This second mystery man might easily have come from the back garden—there were, after all, footprints in that area. But there was no way he could have left the study via the French windows. There was that pesky key, locking the windows on the inside. And then there was the matter of the flowerbeds, which an assailant would have to trample to get out that way. And of course, none of the footprints led anywhere near the house.

"What happened then?" prompted Spector.

"After the men left? I watched the house for a while longer. I assumed one of the chaps must have been Lidia's father. But of course I now know it couldn't have been."

"And?"

"Then Della turned up. I watched her knock on the door and the housekeeper—forget her name—let her in."

"And?"

"Quiet, for a minute or two. Then a loud scream. A woman's scream, from inside the house. So I leapt out of the car and ran round the path to the side of the house."

"So *you* left the second set of footprints," Flint put in.

"Must have done. Before I'd gone a hundred yards, though, a voice from behind me said, 'What the hell do you think you're doing?'"

"Naturally I gave an almighty start. But when I looked I saw it was Lidia. She was standing by the gate. She'd just hopped out of a cab. I ran over to her and kissed her and begged for forgiveness. I said should we go inside, out of the rain, but she said no—she couldn't quite face her father yet."

"So what did you do?"

"We went back to my car. We sat side by side in the coupe for a little while. We didn't say much. It was only when the police arrived that I realised something murky must have happened in the house after all. So we headed inside and acted as if we'd been together all evening at the Palmyra, that we'd only just got out of a cab, and that we'd arrived together."

"No questions asked?"

"Oh, a *lot* of questions asked. But not until the next day. It was then that she told me where she'd been, and that she'd nabbed a painting."

"And what did you say to her?"

"Not much I could say. It didn't seem quite so serious by the light of day, what with her father dead and all. I told her I'd just as soon forget the whole thing ever happened."

"I'm afraid, sir, that may not be possible," said Flint.

"Mr. Bowman," said Spector, "please tell me. *Where is the painting?*"

"I don't know. I swear to you I don't know what she did with it."

Inevitably, their travels brought them back to the Rees house. Olive answered the door wearily. "Is Lidia at home?" Flint asked.

Olive nodded. "In the study."

"Mrs. Turner," Spector said, "before you show us through, I'd like you to do me a favour."

"What's that?"

"Would you look at this photograph for me?" The image he held out to her showed a handsome man, slightly past his prime. There was a superciliousness in his brow, and his widow's peak was a great grey-flecked arc. The housekeeper gave it due consideration. "Do you know this man? Have you ever seen him before?"

Slowly, she leaned in closer to examine the photograph. "No," she said at length. "I haven't. Why? Who is he?"

"You're sure? Please think very carefully."

"I am. And I can tell you for definite I never saw him before in my life."

Spector whipped the photograph away and returned it to his pocket. "Thank you." He did not tell her, but the image was a publicity photograph of Edgar Simmons, the vanished actor. Without another word, she led them through to the study.

"Dr. Rees."

Lidia was at her desk, and did not immediately look up from the papers she was consulting. When she did, Spector noticed her cheeks were coloured slightly. "Usually, when I hear the words 'Dr. Rees,' the person being addressed is my father."

"It must take some getting used to."

She cocked her head pensively. "It did, yes. But I am used to it now. My father's study is now mine. I'll be seeing my first patient tomorrow. And I shall do my very best to help her."

"Della Cookson, by any chance?"

"I can't say. That would breach the doctor-patient privilege, as I'm sure you know."

"Well, I see you've removed your engagement ring."

"You really are quite the detective."

Spector bowed slightly. Deferentially, as though the whole thing embarrassed him. "I'm sorry. It's none of my business. But these old eyes just pick up such things."

"I'm not ashamed of it. My father was right about Marcus, as he was right about everything else. And no matter how I look at it, Marcus betrayed me. I presume you mentioned Della because you know Marcus had been carrying on with her? He treated me like a fool. For a long time I directed my anger at everyone *but* him. I'm now doing my best to remedy that."

"I understand."

She gave a thin smile. "No, you don't. You *think* you do. But that's not the same thing."

"You're trying to honour your father."

"Maybe I am. Yes . . ." she said at length. "Maybe that *is* what I'm doing."

"But there's one aspect of the whole mess which remains unresolved," Spector continued. "The small matter of *El Nacimiento*."

"You mean you haven't found it yet?"

"Let's not be coy about this. I know it was you who took it from Teasel's house. I know you snuck into the party after ditching Marcus at the Palmyra Club. When you arrived back at Dollis Hill, you must have had the painting. So what did you do with it?"

The young doctor smiled. "You know everything else. Seems strange for you not to know that."

"I agree. But it really would be better for you if you told me."

She looked at the two men and smiled a sphinxlike smile.

XIV

HOW TO DISAPPEAR ENTIRELY;
OR, THE PROTEUS CAGE

"We could arrest her, you know," said Flint as they drove away from Dollis Hill.

"Yes, you could. For theft. Not murder."

"Well all right then, after all this back-and-forth, who do *you* think is behind it all?"

"I think . . . perhaps now might be the time for a return visit to Claude Weaver."

When they got to Weaver's house, they were shown in by a maid. Claude was in his attic, apparently hard at work on his latest novel. Rosemary was in the salon, so Flint and Spector joined her. Weaver himself soon emerged when he heard he had visitors.

Flint dispensed with the small talk. "Where were you last night?" he asked Claude pointedly.

"Last night?" Weaver had barely sat down. "You don't mean to tell me some other unfortunate has been slaughtered?"

"Answer the question please, sir."

"I was here. At home. All night."

"Anyone who can vouch for you?"

"My wife."

"It's true, Inspector," said Rosemary. "And I'm not sure I approve of your tone."

"This is a very serious business. I'm afraid I don't have the time or the energy for pleasantries any more. Mr. Weaver, is there anyone *else* who can vouch for your whereabouts last night?"

"No. No, there is not."

Flint's jaw clenched. "I see. Now tell me please, have you ever encountered a young lad by the name of Pete Hobbs?"

"Hobbs? No. The name means nothing to me."

"Perhaps this photograph will jog your memory." Flint produced a photograph of the cadaver. The lad's poor, thin dead face. Eyes sealed shut for the last time.

"Good God," Weaver breathed. Rosemary did not look at the picture.

"Tell me, please. Did you ever meet Hobbs?"

"How . . . how did he die?"

"He was strangled to death. With a length of rope."

"How awful," Rosemary said. She may have been talking to herself.

"No. No, I never met him."

"You're sure? He worked as the elevator boy at Dufresne Court."

"I never met him. I've never been to that building. I'm not a well-travelled man."

"It's true," put in Rosemary. "He wouldn't leave the house if he didn't have to. He's been that way since I married him."

"But my imagination has been my salvation," said Weaver. "It's taken me to wondrous, impossible places."

"Have you ever written about murder?" asked Flint with a slyly arched eyebrow.

"I write about little else. But then, speak to any novelist striving for success on the London literary scene. The public imagination craves blood. Murder means money."

Spector was scanning Weaver's bookshelves. The titles were so lurid they might have dripped from the spines: *Lethal Ascent*, *The Blood-Streaked Idol*, *Peril at Mordlake*, *The Invisible Enemy*. Spector picked a volume at random: *The Devils of Denby*. The cover was a garish swirl of colour, depicting a young woman of waxen beauty cowering in the shadow of some kind of lurid, living gargoyle.

"That was my first," said Weaver, eyeing the cover over the old man's shoulder. "Like all novice efforts it lacks a certain finesse. But it makes up for it in enthusiasm."

"I've read it," said Spector. "I found it very atmospheric. The locations in particular were very well drawn."

Weaver smiled. "Kind of you to say. I get them from photographs. I can look at an image and feel the essence of a place."

"But the fact remains, gentlemen," Rosemary cut in, "that my husband was *here* all night last night. If you don't believe me, you can ask the servants. They'll confirm it gladly."

"I'm sure they will," said Flint, and breezed out of the room.

"This is getting ridiculous now," Flint grumbled on the drive back. "There are too many threads. I can't tie it all together."

"You're right. What we are faced with," Spector said, "is a puzzle with too many pieces. Certain among our clues might connect with others. But taken altogether, as a whole, there are just too many inconsistencies. It's all too ornate and diaphanous." The old magician gave a weary smile. "Oh, Flint. You do come up with some puzzles for me. In a way it's quite wonderful. But in another way . . ." He rubbed his weary eyes.

Spector did not want to return home straight away, so he had Flint drop him off at the Black Pig. He watched as the inspector drove off into the dusk. Then he returned to his customary seat in the snug and dined on a pea and ham pie—a fine repast—and drank a few halves of stout. The thick, tar-like booze fuelled his brain like coal in a locomotive.

Distinctly more cheerful than when he arrived, Joseph Spector left the Black Pig at eight o'clock. It was a short walk through dank, narrow streets to his house in Jubilee Court.

As he approached, he saw that Clotilde had left the porch light aglow for him. Making for the stone steps up to the front door, he became suddenly aware of a thunderous echo of pursuing footsteps—not his own. He did not stop to look.

"Excuse me!"

Still, Spector did not stop.

"Excuse me!"

Finally, with his key not yet in the lock, Spector halted. He turned. Mounting the steps behind him was Claude Weaver. He looked ruffled. Edgy and panicked.

"Mr. Weaver? What are you doing here? Have you been following me?"

"Please, Mr Spector. Let's go inside. I need to talk to you. It's urgent."

Spector unlocked the door and admitted them both to the house.

Weaver was twitchy and agitated as they headed through to the parlour. "Did you lock the front door?" he demanded suddenly.

"Yes, of course."

"So no one can get in?"

"No one. Now. Are you going to tell me what's going on?"

Weaver was panting, his shoulders heaving up and down.

"Take a seat," Spector urged soothingly.

Weaver slumped into an armchair, still panting.

"Let me ring for Clotilde. I'll get you some tea."

"Please. Something stronger."

Spector nodded and produced from the drinks cabinet a cut glass decanter that sparkled in the firelight. He spilled some whisky into a glass, then handed it to Weaver. The novelist downed it in a single motion and sat back in the chair. The colour was finally returning to his face.

"I went to the Black Pig. They gave me your address. Mr. Spector, I need your help. There's someone after me."

"What makes you say that?"

"He's been following me for a while. I don't know who he is. Or what he wants. And you have to understand—I simply couldn't tell you any of this in front of my wife. It must be kept secret. It must. I don't know what I would do if it got out . . ."

"This man—is he out there now?"

Weaver nodded. "But please, don't go and look. Don't let him know I know."

"Describe him."

"I can't see his face. He wears a long black coat and a hat with a wide brim."

"And when did you first notice he was following you?"

"About a week ago."

"I see." Spector thought for a moment. "Wait here." He headed for the door.

"What are you doing?"

"Please. Stay where you are." While the novelist waited anxiously in the parlour, Spector crept back into the hall. He peeked through the curtain. The street was quiet. The lamplighters were at work, piercing the murky dusklight with their torches. But there stood a single unilluminated figure on the far side of the street. He was as Weaver had described: a shadowed figure in a long coat and hat.

Spector withdrew from the window and reached for the telephone. He waited silently while the operator put him through to Scotland Yard. It took perhaps forty seconds for the connection to be made.

"Spector. What is it?" demanded Flint. There was fatigue and tension in his voice.

"I need you to come over here now," said Spector. "And bring some uniforms."

"Why? What is it?"

"Weaver's at my house. And he's got someone with him." Almost as an afterthought, Spector added: "Come to the south entrance. The fellow's watching the house from the front."

"Who is it?"

"We don't know. But he meets Olive's description from the night of the murder. He might also be the one who followed Stenhouse last night."

Flint did not wait to hear more. The line clicked dead.

Spector hung up the phone and returned to the parlour. Weaver sat peering at him expectantly. "Flint is on his way."

"What!" Weaver sprang to his feet.

"Don't worry. We'll get to the bottom of this. He should be here in ten minutes. All we need to do is wait."

"Spector, you don't understand. I don't know who this man is. But I think I know *who* he is, if you catch my meaning . . ."

"You had better tell me."

"I can't! Please. I can't tell anyone. Nobody can find out . . ." He was verging on hysteria.

They spoke in anxious stage whispers, as though the man across the street might hear them. When the tap came at the kitchen door, they both jumped. Spector shuffled to the back of the house and quietly admitted Inspector Flint. "I have men at the entry to Jubilee Court. They're waiting for my signal."

"Good," said Spector. "Come through here."

He led Flint through the house, past a frozen Claude Weaver, and out into the hall. He directed him to the curtain. "You see him?"

Flint leaned in so his nose prodded the glass. "I see him," he said. "Now we don't want this fellow slipping the net again."

"You think he's the one who shot at you at Dufresne Court?"

"Well, I can't be sure. Take me upstairs. I'd better give the signal to my men."

Spector led Flint up the narrow, creaking staircase to the spare room, which looked out on the rear of the house. There, Flint produced from his pocket a cigarette lighter. With his chubby, callused thumb he struck it, and the small bead of orange light flared briefly. "Come on, back round the front," he whispered.

Spector stole a glance out at Jubilee Court from the landing window. The man in black was still there, still waiting, a sinister silhouette. But he did not know the darkness was closing in on him. "I'd advise you to keep your head down," said Flint as he made his way down the stairs. "Could get messy."

But Spector remained on the landing. He watched as the officers closed in on the man with the long black coat. Finally, the chilly silence was pierced by the shrill peal of Flint's whistle. And the officers pounced.

The man bolted. But the uniforms were too quick for him. They tackled him to the ground and one of the constables, Druitt, squatted on his chest. When he was fully subdued, Flint and Spector emerged from the house. Claude Weaver followed, looking shaky, as though he might crumple.

"Hey! What is this!" the man roared as the oxygen was squeezed out of him. His hat rolled away, revealing a smooth, young face. He was perhaps twenty.

Inspector Flint stood over him. "Well, well. We've been looking for you for quite some time, young fellow." He looked to the constables. "Get him on his feet please, gentlemen."

They hoisted him from the ground, each man taking an arm. He was a stranger. Someone neither Flint nor Spector had encountered before. He was clean-shaven and a little shady looking, but otherwise entirely nondescript.

"Who are you? What are you doing here?"

"I'm working. I'm on a job."

"Do you have credentials?"

"My name is Walter Graves. I'm an investigator."

"Did you visit the home of Dr. Anselm Rees on the night of the twelfth?"

The young man's eyes grew wide. "What? How did you know that?"

"And you've been following Claude Weaver?"

"Look, you've no right to do any of this."

"Tell us the truth. Somebody hired you, did they? Is that it? You'd better tell us."

"You have no right to ask me these questions, police or no police. I know my rights. This is all aboveboard. I've got a licence."

Flint turned to Claude Weaver, who was on the verge of collapse. "I suppose this *is* the fellow who's been following you?"

Weaver, struck dumb, simply nodded.

"Very well," said Flint, turning back to the beleaguered investigator. "So. Who hired you?"

"I've already told you. My name is Walter Graves. I work for the Wallace Enquiries Agency."

Stepping toward the fellow with an air of menace, Flint repeated: "And who hired you?"

"You have no right to ask me that. I've not broken the law. I'm a workingman, same as you."

One of the constables tightened his grip on the fellow's arm, wrenching it behind his back. Graves let out a cry.

"Constable!" Flint barked. "I won't have violence under my command. Mr. Graves is absolutely right. We shall obtain a warrant. These documents all appear to be in order." He handed them back. Scowling, the fellow secreted them once again in his jacket. "If you won't disclose your client's identity voluntarily, then the law will compel you to do so. But there *is* something you can tell us. You can tell us what you saw the night Rees died."

"Died? I don't know anything about that. My job was to follow Claude Weaver. And that's what I did."

"What about Floyd Stenhouse? Did you go to his apartment last night? Dufresne Court? Or maybe you'd feel happier talking about it at the Yard?"

"Look, I was hired to follow Claude Weaver. And *only* Claude Weaver. Understand?"

"I'm going to ask you one more time. What was your connection to Anselm Rees? Was he the one who hired you?"

"No. It wasn't a doctor that hired me."

"You realise this is going to be trouble for you, don't you?"

The investigator's shoulders were slumped, resigned. "All she wanted us to do was follow him. Nothing illegal. Nothing untoward."

"Who is it? Who's the client?"

"I can't tell you that," he said forlornly.

Spector presented his open palm. Then he closed it tight and, once more unfurling his fingers, a folded pound note was revealed there. "Who's the client?" he repeated gently.

The investigator snatched up the note and slipped it into the inside pocket of his overcoat. "The police are looking the wrong way with this. There's nothing for them to see. His wife wanted him followed, that's all. She thinks he's playing the field."

Spector looked at Weaver and realised this revelation was exactly what the novelist had feared all along. "Mrs. Weaver hired you?"

"That's what I said, didn't I?"

"And you've followed him for two weeks?"

"That I have. I can tell you now that whatever's on Mr. Weaver's mind, it's certainly not murder."

"How do you know?"

"Because I've been watching him the entire time."

"So you followed him when he went to the Rees house?"

"On the twelfth? Yes."

"He *did* go there that night?"

"That's what I said, didn't I? When he left the restaurant it was the first place he headed."

"I . . ." Weaver was beginning to sweat. Spector and Flint ignored him and carried on their inquisition.

"When did he arrive?"

"Eleven fifteen. He rang the front doorbell. I watched him go in."

Flint and Spector looked at each other. Eleven fifteen. That was when the phantom visitor appeared on the doorstep. But it couldn't have been Weaver, because Mrs. Turner would have recognised him. Wouldn't she? She had met Weaver plenty of times, hadn't she?

"Then what happened, Mr. Graves?"

"Well, I had to see what went on in the house. So I crept round the back via the side gate."

"Wait a moment. So you were in the rear garden of the Rees house that night?"

"Yes. I was. And I could see through the French windows into the study."

Weaver looked about to collapse.

"How close to the house were you?"

"Not very."

"Close enough to leave footprints in the six feet of flowerbeds?"

The investigator shook his head. "I was under a tree at the bottom of the garden, sheltering from the rain. But the room was well lit, so I could see straight in."

"You saw Dr. Rees?"

"Of course I did. I saw him let Weaver into the study, and then they sat and chatted for a few minutes."

"What happened then?"

"Weaver left. I didn't stick around—I hopped back over the wall and picked up Weaver's trail again."

"But Rees was alive when you left?"

"Of course he was!"

Spector considered this closely. "Could you make out anything they were talking about?"

"No. But they were friendly, far as I could tell. They drank."

"Drank?"

"He poured it out of one of those glass . . . what do you call it?"

"Decanter. Who poured it?"

"Rees did. The doctor. It looked like whisky."

"Did they both drink?"

The investigator nodded. And that was when Claude Weaver collapsed. He simply keeled over sideways without warning. Spector surveyed the fallen author dispassionately.

"Better get him inside," said Flint. Two constables hoisted his unconscious body across the threshold of Spector's home and vanished from view.

"Well," said Spector. "This changes things."

"You can say that again," Flint replied. "I've gone from clueless to completely hornswoggled."

"Really?" Spector was smiling. "I should have thought this made things a lot clearer."

Flint moaned exasperatedly. "You're free to go, Mr. Graves. But we'll need a statement from you tomorrow."

When the excitement had died down and Flint and Spector were again alone in twilit Jubilee Court, the inspector demanded: "And just what do you think this all means, then? Surely it proves the killer had to be Claude Weaver."

"I think it proves the opposite."

Flint scowled. "From what Graves described, Weaver was the mysterious visitor Olive Turner told us about. She must have got it wrong when she said she didn't recognise him. Obviously she's not the infallible witness we thought she was. He was in the doctor's study from eleven till eleven forty-five. But *why* didn't she recognise him? Was he disguised?"

"I think the answer is a lot simpler than that, Inspector. I think she told us she had never seen him before because she really *hadn't* seen him before."

"But Claude Weaver was a regular patient. She'd met all three patients plenty of times."

"Yes," Spector's smile stretched ecstatically. "Isn't it a marvellous trick? I think for all his secrecy and skulduggery, Claude Weaver is actually quite an unfortunate man. You see, he has tried very hard to maintain a certain way of life, only for it to prove unsustainable. That, if anything, is his only crime. It was a bad bout of luck which beset him the night Rees was killed. Forget about the publisher's assertion that Weaver *saw* something which upset him and sent him reeling from the restaurant. We know there was nothing for him to see. But what were they discussing?"

Flint flipped back through his notebook. "Paperbacks or some such nonsense."

"Right. And the words conveniently reported to us by the publisher were "the literati will know the difference between a real Claude Weaver and a fake one.""

"And *that's* what sent him stumbling off into the night?"

"Those words were an epiphany to him."

"What?"

Spector didn't answer. "There's something that still troubles me about Floyd Stenhouse's dream. If I can make it fit, then I can make the whole thing fit. What I mean is that I think there may be something else about these dreams, something beyond the superficial symbolism. Answer me this: when Floyd Stenhouse called Anselm Rees on the night of the twelfth, what did Rees do?"

"Told him off for calling so late."

"Yes. And?"

"And he listened to the dream anyway."

"Good. And?"

"And . . ." Flint mused, "and he wrote it down."

"That's it!" the old man snapped his fingers. "Olive Turner heard the scratching of Rees's pen as he wrote down Stenhouse's dream. Which means . . ."

"What happened to the notes?"

"Exactly. If Rees noted down what Stenhouse said to him, where did the notes go? Presumably, the killer took them. But why? Maybe something in the dream itself was incriminating somehow? It seems bizarre—outright impossible—but why else would those pages be gone?" Spector beamed. Wheels were turning. "Something else was gone too. Think about what Olive Turner told us about the doctor's study, and what was found on the dead man's desk when the police finally got there."

"I'm thinking."

"All right, I'll give you a clue. Walter Graves couldn't see much from his vantage point between the trees. But there was *one* detail he was able to make out. What was it?"

It was Flint's turn to glow with revelation. "Drinks. They were drinking."

"He poured them both drinks from the crystal decanter. But when the police arrived, there was only *one* tumbler on the desk. Only one tumbler in the entire study. And they searched everywhere, didn't they? So where did the second tumbler go?"

Flint scrutinised his shoes. "Why would the killer take one of the tumblers?"

"Maybe the same reason he tore out the pages dealing with Stenhouse's dream. Figure out the reasoning behind one, and you'll probably get the other too."

"You've got it, haven't you, Spector? Care to give me a hint?"

"Not yet. But soon, Flint. I need to make a few arrangements."

"For what?"

Spector's pale eyes sparkled in the lamplight. "For the big finish."

INTERLUDE

WHEREIN THE READER'S ATTENTION

IS RESPECTFULLY REQUESTED

O nce upon a time, this would be the point in the narrative where a challenge is issued to the reader. "All the data are in front of you," I would say, "that you will need to identify the murderer of Dr. Anselm Rees and Pete Hobbs, as well as the means by which those murders were accomplished."

These days such practices are antiquated and rather passé. But who am I to stand in the way of a reader's fun? It's true that all the evidence is there, and in plain sight too. If there are any would-be sleuths among you, now is the time to make yourselves known. There is no prize, material or otherwise, save the quiet glory of having triumphed at what a wise man once termed "the grandest game in the world."

Thursday, September 17, 1936

XV

ONE LAST TRICK

J oseph Spector had a very specific set of instructions. In the first instance, they required George Flint to be available from nine a.m. Bleary-eyed and irritable, the inspector got to the Rees house in Dollis Hill just after five past. Jerome Hook was with him, and the door was answered by Spector himself.

"Ah. Gentlemen. So glad you could be here," he told them sardonically.

"Spector, what's going on? What are we doing here?"

"Come in, come in, quickly."

They headed into the hallway. "What's going on here?"

"There are guests arriving shortly. But currently we have the run of the place. Lidia Rees has spent the night at the Dorchester Hotel. And Olive Turner has agreed to stay with her sister." He led them through to the rear of the house, to the kitchen. "If you'd be so good as to wait here. If I've timed everything correctly, then Floyd Stenhouse should be the first to arrive."

Flint and Hook shared an uncomfortable glance. In spite of everything, Flint could not quite bring himself to trust this old man.

Stenhouse was indeed the first to arrive. He was his usual twitchy self, and Spector took him through to the lounge where, strangely enough, a metal birdcage stood on a small wooden table.

"Mr Spector, what's all this about? I'm happy to do whatever I can to help find the doctor's killer, but . . ."

"This is Proteus," said Spector, indicating the cage. "I call him that because he lives in a Proteus Cage. And because, like Proteus, he is famed for his malleability, flexibility, and adaptability." With his left hand he held up the cage. Through its narrow bars was visible a small, beautiful yellow bird.

"He has a mate, of course—I cannot bear the thought of such a creature imprisoned forever alone—but for our purposes Proteus will suffice. Please, feel free to examine him. And the cage, of course."

Stenhouse leaned forward and peered at the bird, which peered imperiously back, cocking its head. "Flexibility?" Stenhouse repeated.

"Of course. He can disappear at will. See?" And with a click of the old man's fingers, the bird vanished.

The young musician now sat bolt upright, his eyes wide and glassy. "What have you done with him?"

"Nothing at all. As I told you, the power is entirely his own. He will come back when he is ready."

With that, Spector clicked his fingers once more and the bird returned. "Please—examine the cage if you like."

Stenhouse did so, staring bemusedly at the little bird. "But—where did he go?"

Spector gave a soft chuckle, delighting in the young man's rancour. "Delightful little trick, isn't it? And quite baffling. But devilishly simple when you hold it up to anything other than the most basic scrutiny. The whole thing lies in the cage, of course. The bird never moves. But the top and bottom of the cage are fitted with mirrors. With a little basic misdirection—for example, clicking one's fingers—the trickster may simply twist the cornice on the top of the cage, moving the mirrors so that they obstruct the bird but give a perfect view of the curtain beyond."

Now he shrugged, and Stenhouse sank back into his seat. "Rather pedestrian, I think you'll agree."

Stenhouse gave an embarrassed chuckle. "You fooled me completely."

"I'm not sure if I believe you," said Spector. "I think you are just being kind to an old man. After all, it's an ancient trick. It dates back thousands of years. True, this is a particularly beautiful example of the species . . ."

"No need to be modest, Spector. We must all accept our strengths as well as our weaknesses. As a musician, I am a genius. As a conjuror, sir, you are the same."

Now Spector laughed. "Well, I've had worse reviews," he said. "But there is a serious point to be made. You see, I have shown just one of the many, many methods by which a human body—alive or dead—may vanish from a locked room."

Flint watched this discreetly through the lounge doorway. He had learned nothing new.

Lidia Rees came home soon after that, and with her was Olive Turner. The two women had met for morning coffee at the Dorchester before returning home for Joseph Spector's little demonstration. Neither seemed especially enthusiastic about the birdcage, or about Floyd Stenhouse.

The next car to arrive was Marcus Bowman's; the throb of the engine could be heard all the way down Dollis Hill. Bowman was admitted by Sergeant Hook, swaggering over the threshold in surly silence. When he stepped into the drawing room, Lidia glanced at him once, then looked away. He did not speak, and sat on the far side of the room.

"Thank you for coming, Mr. Bowman," said Spector, the venerable host. "We shan't keep you long. And who knows? You might learn something."

Flint hovered in the hallway, his pipe pluming smoke. While Spector was settling himself into the role of host, the inspector was all about the business. He was also flanked by two constables, who discreetly secured the room.

Next to arrive was Della Cookson. Introductions were made, and Patients A and B began to get to know one another. Their small talk was pained and awkward, but Joseph Spector hung on to every word. Lidia sat, statuesque in the chilly sunlight. Marcus Bowman fidgeted like an infant, scratching his knee, licking his lips, gently flicking a forelock away from his forehead. But his gaze was fixed on the floor, and he did not register the arrival of the new guests.

Spector stood at the front of the room and cleared his throat. "Ladies and gentlemen, I am pleased you have had the opportunity to get to know my good friend Proteus. Before I commence with the main event, I should like to demonstrate a very minor illusion." He presented them with an elegantly fanned-out deck of cards. "Miss Cookson, please pick one."

Nervously, the actress stepped forward and did so.

"Now show it to the others."

She did. Flint craned his neck to see: Three of Clubs.

"Good," said Spector. Then he took the card from her and held it up. "Now, watch closely."

They studied the card between his fingers. He held it aloft for a moment like some paganistic totem. Then—snap!—it transformed before their eyes.

There were gasps from the assembled company. Then a moment of bemused silence. The card had transmogrified into a small, square sepia-tinged photograph. It was a portrait of a young woman, perhaps twenty years of age. Flint had never seen her before.

Spector, still holding the photograph above his head, smiled. "Does anybody recognise this young lady?"

Silence.

The smile slowly dissolved from Spector's face. When he spoke, there was ice in his voice. "Somebody does."

He handed the photograph to Della, and it was passed around the guests. They all exchanged nervous and confused glances.

"Her name is Frieda Tanzer," said Spector, "and she is the reason we are gathered here today."

"Who else are we waiting for, Spector?" Flint called out from the hallway.

"Just the Weavers."

"In that case, I think they're here."

"Excellent." Spector scuttled, spiderlike, to the window and peered into the street. Right enough, a taxicab had drawn to a halt and Mrs. Weaver was stepping out. Spector headed for the hall.

Before they could ring the bell, Spector opened the front door. Claude Weaver looked pale, evidently still suffering the aftereffects of last night's adventure. His face was a mask.

Spector led the couple through. Sergeant Hook held the door open for them. Nobody else knew it, but Spector was more nervous now than he had been at any point during this case. As far as he was concerned, it was the culmination of his efforts.

The effect of the couple's arrival was like a thunderclap. All eyes turned toward them. And Claude Weaver looked at each person in turn. His gaze settled on one of the guests. "What's going on here?" he cried. "Is this another of your tricks, Spector?"

"I'm afraid not," said Spector. "I'm afraid it's very real."

The one Weaver was looking at was Floyd Stenhouse.

Stenhouse, who seemed rooted to his seat, did not say a word. He fixed Weaver with a steady glare. He looked like a predator ready to strike.

"Mr. Weaver, will you please identify this man?" Spector said.

"Well . . ." Weaver stumbled over his words. His wife, Rosemary, stood at his side, and took his arm. Weaver cleared his throat and then, in a clear, strident voice said: "That's Anselm Rees."

Stenhouse's shoulders slumped. Before he could move, Sergeant Hook was in the doorway, blocking any means of exit. Stenhouse snorted. "You don't have to worry, gentlemen," he said. "I won't give you any trouble." And he let himself be handcuffed.

"It's an understandable mistake to make," said Spector. "Especially considering the fact you two have only met once before—the night Rees was murdered. We knew that you, Mr. Weaver, were the mysterious visitor. But what we did not stop to consider was the fact that the man you met that night was *not* Dr. Rees. That perhaps the real Dr. Rees lay unconscious in that infamous teakwood trunk, and the man who spoke to you was actually his murderer."

"Now hold on," Flint said, "that doesn't make any sense."

"It will," Spector went on. "If you'll allow me, I will go right back to the beginning."

"Claude Weaver, like a lot of married men, is having an affair. But *unlike* a lot of married men he is in a unique position.

Namely, a position of anonymity. He is a famous recluse—a contradiction in terms, perhaps. But many people know the name while very few know the face. This gave him a degree of licence. But of course, his wife grew suspicious. So he invented a 'mental disorder'—the fugue states which he could lapse into whenever he was unable to account for his whereabouts. And Mrs. Weaver unwittingly played into his hands. She called his bluff, and arranged for him to see a psychiatrist."

"This is scandalous!" cried Rosemary Weaver. But Flint noticed she was no longer clutching her husband's arm.

"You've lost me there, Spector. How did she play into his hands?"

"She arranged a weekly appointment where Claude would be out of her house, away from her critical gaze."

"Yes, but of course Rees would have told her if Claude had failed to turn up for an appointment. Or even if he was a few minutes late."

"Right. But you're forgetting that Claude Weaver is a master plotter. He agreed to keep the appointment—maintaining the fallacy that he feared for his own mental state—but then he set wheels in motion. Truly, it could have been *anyone* who turned up at the house in Dollis Hill for that first appointment. And it could have been anyone who established himself as Patient C. And, believe it or not, it was. What Claude Weaver did was to enlist the aid of an underemployed stage actor to *impersonate* him during the encounters with Anselm Rees, leaving him free to conduct his illicit liaisons untroubled by the gaze of his wife."

"Underemployed actor . . ." repeated Della Cookson. "Are you talking about Edgar Simmons?"

"The very same. And this Edgar Simmons now seems to have disappeared very hastily. Left the country, I should imagine. Almost as though he had been paid off, don't you think?"

"So wait," said Flint. "Whenever Anselm Rees spoke about 'Patient C' or 'Claude Weaver,' he was really talking about the impostor, about this Edgar Simmons?"

"Precisely. To maintain consistency, the actor and Weaver would hold regular debriefs, to ensure that Weaver was up to speed on what had been discussed in the sessions. It seemed like the perfect plan. And really, it was! After all, it worked for a long time. But inevitably, Mrs. Weaver's suspicions came creeping back. She found that the mere knowledge that Claude was undergoing treatment with the finest psychiatrist in the world was not enough to assuage her concerns. So she decided to take extra steps. She approached the Wallace Agency, and she arranged to have her husband followed by an investigator named Walter Graves.

"It was only the week of the murder that Claude Weaver finally became conscious of Graves's presence on his trail. This ratcheted up his paranoia, sent him reeling into a state of near psychosis. For you see, he did not know what he would do if his secret was ever revealed.

"This also meant there was a patient of Dr. Rees's who identified himself as Claude Weaver, and whom the household came to take for Claude Weaver. But he *was not* Claude Weaver.

"The real Weaver knew the investigator would eventually come to question Dr. Rees, and soon the whole game would be up. He was quick to pay off Edgar Simmons, to get him out of the way. But he felt trapped, as though the walls were closing in on him. And it was in that frame of mind that he went to dinner with his publisher on the night of the twelfth."

"What are you accusing me of?" Claude Weaver's face had turned beige.

"Only duplicity and infidelity, Mr. Weaver. Which I think you'll agree are lesser crimes than murder."

Spector went on: "In your troubled state of mind, all it took was a discussion with your publisher about 'fake Weavers' to set you off. You stumbled out of the restaurant in a state of complete apoplexy. You decided to head to Dollis Hill in a last-ditch attempt to reason with Dr. Rees, to explain your situation and beg for clemency. Maybe even to pay *him* off too. So you arrived here that night without having met Dr. Rees before. Or, indeed, Olive Turner, who was greatly troubled by your secretive manner. But what you did not know when you walked into the study that night was that you were interrupting an elaborate murder plot which was already in progress. Because your visit was entirely unplanned, wasn't it? Rees was not expecting you. Or rather, he was not expecting *you*. In fact, the visitor he was expecting was none other than Patient A, Floyd Stenhouse. You see, when he was touring Austria with the Philharmonic some years ago, Mr. Stenhouse met the Snakeman's daughter."

"Frieda Tanzer," Stenhouse said with difficulty, "was the love of my life. It was only after she killed herself that I found out about her father, and Dr. Rees's reckless treatment which led directly to her own suicide. But what can I say? Some grudges do not go away with time."

Spector again seized the reins. "So we have the first problem—how did the killer get into the study? This was the simplest aspect of the whole thing. No one came in by the front door. We know the rain started at around eleven o'clock, so we assumed no one could have come in via the windows because we found no footprints in the wet flowerbed. Because the murder did not occur until eleven forty-five, we guessed the murderer must have got in *after* the rain started. But what if he was in there all along? Rees was expecting a visitor—we can assume that this was Stenhouse, who had made an appointment under conditions of utmost secrecy. I imagine he told Rees he knew about the circumstances of Der Schlangenmann's death and that he intended to use them to disgrace the good doctor. Something along those lines, something sensitive. That was why Rees instructed Olive Turner *not* to show the visitor in. He did not want to risk her overhearing any of their conversation.

"But of course, Stenhouse caught Rees unawares by arriving early, and via the rear garden instead of the front door. This was *before* eleven o'clock, when the rain started, so he left no trace in the flowerbed. Rees admitted his killer to the study via the windows.

"Then he served drinks—whisky from the decanter. He poured out two tumblers. It was an easy enough sleight of hand for the killer to add a sleeping draught to his own glass and then, during a moment of misdirection, to swap the glasses. Soon enough his intended victim sipped the whisky, and slipped closer to unconsciousness. Dr. Rees's limbs were paralysed, and he no doubt realised the fate that awaited him. But of course, the killer took immense delight in watching the old man suffer.

"By this point, I imagine the rain was tumbling down—it was perhaps nearing eleven forty-five. I picture the killer unfurling the razor and readying himself to commit his symbolic act of vengeance. But then, imagine the horror in his heart when he heard a sudden knock at the door. Quickly, he returned the razor to his pocket and deposited the unconscious Anselm Rees in the large wooden chest. His visitor, of course, was Claude Weaver. The *real* Claude Weaver. Who we now know had never actually met Anselm Rees—not once. And so it was natural enough for Weaver to assume that the man in the study *was* Anselm Rees.

"I imagine the discussion going something like this—'You don't know me, Dr. Rees, but I have a favour to ask of you.' The killer realised two things almost instantly: one, that his visitor had mistaken him for Rees, and two, that the reason for his visit was compromising. In other words, even though he knew his plan had been endangered, he still retained the upper hand. So he took his unwitting stooge into the study, and listened to his story of deceit and infidelity. Already a plan was forming, an idea that he might possibly frame this fellow for the murder he had not yet committed. So he poured him a drink—using the undrugged tumbler, of course—and listened to his confession.

"When their consultation was over (let's not forget that Weaver truly believed he was talking to Rees), Stenhouse let poor, deluded Weaver out of the study and into the hall. Weaver in turn let himself out of the house by the front door (observed by Olive Turner) and disappeared into the night. So, the killer was once again locked in the study alone with his victim. He heaved the unconscious doctor out of the chest and deposited him once again in the chair (he did this unobserved because Walter Graves, who had been watching outside, had followed his quarry elsewhere, off into the night). At this point, he wasted no more time. He took the razor and slaughtered the unconscious Anselm Rees where he sat.

"He could have left the office then, and all would have been well. But then he remembered the part of the plan he had put in place to establish his own alibi: the telephone call. At that moment, the phone on the desk rang. This was Pete Hobbs, who had been paid by Stenhouse to help him sneak out of Dufresne Court, and to call the appointed number at the appointed time in order to establish an alibi. Of course, the lad wasn't to know there was murder involved. So Stenhouse answered the desk telephone in character as Rees, impersonating his voice and conducted his half of a conversation with himself. He scribbled on the pad to add verisimilitude, but realised too late that his handwriting would not match Rees's. So when the conversation was concluded and he had hung up, he tore out the pages.

"Now he knew he had to act quickly. He'd established an alibi for himself—assuming he could rely on the elevator boy's silence—but he still had to extricate himself from the room. He was about to leave via the hall door when he heard Olive admitting Della Cookson to the house and approaching the door. Now he was in a bind—Rees was dead, so he couldn't continue to impersonate him. And these two women were desperate to get into that study. So he headed for the French windows. On opening them, he realised he would not be able to escape this way, as he would inevitably leave footprints in the flowerbed. But there was a narrow stone step beyond the window, a tiny alcove* where (by forcing himself into the darkened corner) Stenhouse could conceal himself. So he was outside the house, but he did not step onto the flowerbed."

"Then how did he manage to leave the French windows locked on the inside?"

"He didn't. It's a basic trick. The key was in the lock on the inside, and the ladies were unable to open the windows when they rattled the handle, so they *assumed* the windows must be locked.** But in fact, they were not. Stenhouse simply used a cord of some description—perhaps even his necktie—to loop around the twin door handles, and pulling it tight, he created the illusion that the windows were locked on the inside. Once they had tried the handles, and satisfied themselves that the windows were locked, the ladies turned their attention inward, to the room itself. So Stenhouse could peer through the glass and observe when the coast was clear. He only had to wait a few

---

*   See page 11.
**   See page 42.

minutes before Della and Olive headed out into the kitchen. Then he could reenter the study (locking the windows behind him) and tiptoe out into the hall, exiting via the unlocked front door while the two ladies were plying themselves with brandy. Any sounds he made would naturally be covered by the heavy rainfall."

"Well I'll be damned," said Flint.

"But unfortunately, Floyd Stenhouse had not got away as cleanly as he thought. There was Pete Hobbs, the one person who might put two and two together and ruin his carefully wrought alibi. I think all along you knew you would have to kill Pete, didn't you?"

Stenhouse looked very pleased with himself. "Yes, I rather think I did."

"So now we come to that very messy business at Dufresne Court. By the time Anselm Rees was dead, Stenhouse was probably already planning his second murder. What's that line from *Macbeth*? 'I am in blood stepped in so far that, should I wade no more, returning were as tedious as go o'er.'"

"But unlike the first murder, there were two pieces of preparation Stenhouse needed to make in order to pull off the elevator trick. One was the doorbell, the other was the elevator itself. Let's take the doorbell first: our industrious Mr. Stenhouse gimmicked it so that it would ring automatically at an appointed time."

"Ah-*ha*," said Flint, triumphantly, "I *knew* there was something iffy about what happened with Bream. The bell rang and he went to see who it was, but there was no one there. That was because it was *Stenhouse* who rang the bell from inside the apartment. Right?"

"In a way. Let me explain: when I visited the apartment myself I noticed a seemingly innocuous alarm clock by the window.* In fact, Stenhouse was likely already using this to experiment with his plan. As you may or may not know, a common mechanical alarm clock stores energy thanks to a coiled spring mechanism. Using this same principle, our killer was able to rig the doorbell. He disconnected the bell from its wiring, removed its electrical innards and replaced them with the compact gears and springs of the alarm clock. Fortunately for him, the two systems are not dissimilar—though the doorbell obviously does not have a clock face, it has a clapper which may be connected to the mainspring. Once the device was in place, all he needed to do was to remove the bell, wind the mechanism, replace the bell, then wait. The length of time until the bell rang could be determined by how tightly he wound the spring. I presume that is why he was a little slow in answering your knock—he was gauging how much time he would need to enact his plan, and then winding the mechanism accordingly. He gave himself five minutes.

"And then, while Flint and Harrow were away, and while Constable Bream's attention was directed at the corridor by the ringing doorbell, Stenhouse took the opportunity to retrieve his concealed revolver (snared in a handkerchief to avoid fingerprints) and to drop it from the apartment window

---

* See page 89.

down into the courtyard below. The pistol was on a hair trigger, and so when it hit the ground it fired a bullet. This was the shot that unfortunately injured Bill Harper."

"Why did he do *that*?" said Della Cookson.

"To put the police at panic stations. He wanted the conditions to be perfect when they discovered Pete Hobbs's corpse. And also, it helped to distance himself from the attack. He had a perfect alibi after all, snug in his apartment with a police guard, no less."

"I think you'd better tell us," said Flint, "just how Pete Hobbs was killed."

Spector nodded solemnly. "I mentioned two pieces of preparation, the doorbell being the first. Well, the second was the elevator. Have any of you ever heard of a 'vampire trap?'"

"I have," said Della.

"I thought you might. It's a theatrical term for a very specific type of trapdoor. It derives its name from its first appearance onstage in an adaptation of Polidori's "The Vampyre"—it is a trapdoor held in place by spring leaves which part when pressure is applied and then immediately reseal. That is the same effect he sought to achieve with the elevator ceiling hatch—for the trapdoor to fall open under the corpse's weight, then for it to *reseal itself afterward.*

"To accomplish this, he took a sheet of Indian rubber and nailed it into place covering both the hatch and the hinge on which it swung. This would not have taken him long—he could have done it at any point when Pete was on one of his 'cigarette breaks,' which the desk clerk said could last up to an hour. All he would need to do was to paint over it so that it was not immediately noticeable—the recent repairs would account for the smell of wet paint. I'm sure I don't need to remind you that both the rubber and the paint were in evidence at Stenhouse's apartment when we first visited him.* And this was the only gimmick he needed to work the elevator trick.

"Next he invited Hobbs up to his apartment. During this meeting—which must have taken place at around six thirty—he fed him a drugged drink which sent him spiralling into unconsciousness. Now, we know that the fifth floor of the apartment building is unoccupied. So all Stenhouse had to do was wait until the corridor between his own apartment and the elevator was clear. It was then a matter of carrying the boy to the elevator and travelling up to the fifth floor. He would also need to ensure the hatch was unbolted. Next, he sent the elevator back down to the fourth floor, while he and the unconscious Hobbs *remained* on the fifth floor. Then he prised open the cage and he had access to the roof of the elevator itself.

"It was comparatively simple for him to loop a cord loosely around the unfortunate boy's neck and tie the other end to the elevator cage. Then he headed back down the stairs to his apartment to call Inspector Flint with his made-up tale of a mysterious stranger (evidently playing on the account Olive Turner had given to police at Dollis Hill). And when the police arrived, there was someone there at all times to account for Stenhouse's

---

* See page 89.

whereabouts. It was essentially a remotely activated murder. When Flint took the elevator down again, the cord round the boy's neck would tighten and finish him off, leaving him hanging in the elevator shaft and creating the illusion that he had been murdered at a time when Stenhouse was under police guard. The cord had also been sufficiently frayed beforehand that with the weight of Pete's body pulling on it, it would eventually snap and he would tumble down onto the roof of the elevator again. This would cause the body to drop *through* the large square trapdoor feet-first, landing inside the elevator itself. This gave the appearance that Hobbs had been killed on the ground floor and his body somehow deposited in the elevator there.

"The only anomaly here is the trapdoor in the ceiling. Though it was certainly *large* enough for a body to drop through, this would have caused the trapdoor itself to hang open. No doubt you would have noticed it swinging above your heads. That is why he rigged it with the Indian rubber, effectively turning it into a vampire trap. The rubber held the hatch in place, giving the illusion that it was closed and bolted, but allowing it to buckle under the weight of the dropping corpse. And when the corpse was safely inside the elevator, the stiff and sturdy rubber regained its original shape and pushed the thin wooden trapdoor back into place.

"He made sure to be present at the moment the corpse was discovered, and whilst the three policemen examined the corpse and Della Cookson turned away in horror,* he took the

---

* See page 178.

opportunity to quickly rebolt the hatch, so that any examination would yield an apparently hermetically sealed elevator. And the only evidence of his crime was the cord tied to the fifth-floor elevator cage and the strip of rubber. I am sure that both of these have now been destroyed."

Nobody spoke for a while. Eventually, it was Marcus Bowman who broke the silence. "Well, that explains everything, doesn't it?"

"Not quite," said Flint. "It wraps up the two murders very neatly. But it doesn't tell us the whereabouts of the stolen painting, *El Nacimiento*."

"Oh *that*," said Spector. "That was really the simplest aspect of the whole thing . . ."

But before he could explain, something happened. Stenhouse, who had stood handcuffed throughout the unpicking of his elaborate crimes, reached surreptitiously into his jacket. With a flick of the wrist, he produced a straight razor.

It was such a swift motion that it took the rest of the assembled company a moment to realise exactly what was happening. And by then, the blade was at Della Cookson's pulsing jugular.

"Inspector Flint," he said, "I will need you to remove your constables from the hallway. Miss Cookson and I are going for a drive. I noticed a yellow car in the road outside. To whom does it belong?"

Bowman, who had been gaping at the spectacle of sudden violence, looked at the floor.

"Marcus," said Lidia, "my *ex*-fiancé."

"Give me the keys, Mr. Bowman."

Bowman stood up to do so, and as he proffered the key ring Spector noted a tremor in his hand. Stenhouse took the keys and forced Della toward the door.

"Don't be stupid now," said Flint.

Spector watched from the lounge window as the handcuffed Floyd Stenhouse forced Della Cookson into the yellow coupe and clambered in after her.

Stenhouse stared back at them grimly as Della started up the engine and eased the car away from the kerb. The razor sparkled in the morning sun.

As the car began to pick up speed, Spector and the guests piled out into the street to watch as the killer and his captive roared away. But before the car reached the end of Dollis Hill Road, a gunshot punctured the quiet suburban air. The rear left tyre exploded and the vehicle shrieked sideways, leaving a mad steaming rainbow of burned rubber on the road. Della was thrown clear. But Floyd Stenhouse was not.

The car collided with an iron lamp post, and for a moment the only sound was the dying echo of crunched metal and shattered glass. But then the fuel tank must have sparked. And the guests watched as the coupe burst into flames.

Once it was clear there was nothing to be done for Floyd Stenhouse, everyone's attention turned to the gunman. Claude Weaver, still shaking, relinquished his revolver willingly.

"What's the matter, Spector?" Flint wanted to know.

The two men were back in the lounge of the Rees house, and Olive Turner was heaping sugar into a row of teacups. Everyone's nerves had taken quite a battering.

"I tried to tell you, Flint. If Stenhouse hadn't interrupted us, I was about to explain."

"About the painting?"

"About *El Nacimiento*, exactly. The trick was to consider the circumstances of the night Dr. Rees died—what was *different* about that night, compared to every other night since? When I looked at it from that angle, the solution was obvious."

A pause. "Was it?"

"It was. You see, we know Lidia came straight from Teasel's house back to Dollis Hill, so she must have had the painting with her. But what was *different* about that night was that it was raining. Marcus Bowman snuck round the side of the house, leaving his car unattended.* The car which is now burnt away to a blackened husk. But I assume that Bowman had unfurled its soft canopy roof that night, if only to preserve the upholstery of the back seats from the barrage of rain. Whenever we have seen that car, it has been open topped. But that night, it was covered. So all Lidia had to do was to slide the painting smoothly into the unfurled canopy's housing, and she had got a perfect hiding place."

After a long silence, Flint spoke. "I see," he said. He was looking out the window at the ruined coupe which was now being towed away. And at the genius of Manolito Espina, which coiled upward and away from Dollis Hill in a thick black plume.

---

* See page 207.

EPILOGUE

THE CONJUROR'S TALE

A month after the events at Dollis Hill and the unfortunate death of Floyd Stenhouse, Inspector Flint took Joseph Spector out to dinner. It was quite a feat getting Spector away from the cosy cocoon of the Black Pig, but Flint was the man to do it. They dined at Brown's, where Claude Weaver and his publisher, Tweedy, had dined the night of the Rees murder. On the publisher's recommendation, Flint had the trout.

"How did you settle on Stenhouse as the killer?" the inspector asked. "For my money it might have been any one of them."

"Well," said Spector through a mouthful of brisket, "Stenhouse mentioned that he had toured extensively with the Philharmonic.* He is the only one of our suspects to have done so, therefore he is the likeliest to have encountered Rees elsewhere

---

* See page 88.

in Europe. He mentioned that he had visited Vienna once. That was 1927 or '28. And it was there that he met—and fell in love with—Der Schlangenmann's daughter. She was beautiful, but tortured by what had happened to her father. It was a trauma from which she would never recover. And so, when she took her own life, Floyd Stenhouse knew who to blame. The man he saw as the orchestrator of all his sorrows. Dr. Anselm Rees. The man who drove his lover's father to suicide. His revenge had been brewing for a long time. And when serendipity dropped the unfortunate Dr. Rees into his lap, he was quick to seek him out and establish himself as a patient in dire need of psychiatric treatment. It was all a smokescreen facilitating his revenge."

"What about the dreams, then? Did they mean anything after all?"

"I'm certain they did. In fact, I would say that they presented the answer to the whole puzzle, if we had only known how to look for it."

"You don't think Stenhouse made them up? As an excuse to set up his standing appointment with Rees?"

"Far from it. If anything, I imagine he pared down the dreams to make them more palatable. But he did make one significant amendment. Or rather, substitution. The man with the lamp. He told Rees that it was his father. But I would surmise that the demonic figure of his dream was Anselm Rees himself."

Flint was nodding. "Yes. It fits. Seeing the doctor, who was someone Stenhouse had built up in his imagination to almost biblical proportions; it must have created quite a psychological reaction, seeing him in the flesh that first time."

They were enjoying their after-dinner coffees when that familiar mischievous glint returned to Spector's pale eyes.

"A last little trick for you, Flint. Before we call it a night. Observe as I read the waiter's mind." Spector produced the folded handkerchief from his breast pocket and presented it to the waiter. From that same pocket, he produced a pen, which he also handed to the waiter.

"Now, young man, please take the handkerchief and pen over to the counter. And I need you to think of a number between one and fifty. And you must write that number on the handkerchief. Understand?"

The young waiter, eyes as wide and gleaming as dinner plates, nodded. Spector turned his back as the waiter wrote down his number and folded the handkerchief. Then the two men faced each other again.

Spector narrowed his eyes at the bemused fellow. "Your number is thirty-seven."

The waiter, blinking, unfurled the handkerchief. Emblazoned there in blue ink was the legend: "37."

Spector smiled and presented him with a silver coin. "Thank you, young man."

"Now that was remarkable," said Flint. "Just how do you do a trick like that?"

"It's what we call impromptu magic. Because, you see, it doesn't require a stage and a curtain and a top hat. You can do it anywhere."

"But how is it *done*?"

With a modest incline of his head, Spector said: "The whole thing's pure humbug, of course. That pen doesn't even have any ink. The handkerchief I handed to the waiter was already printed with the number 37. When he unfolded it, he found concealed inside it a silver sovereign. Which is no doubt in his pocket as we speak. The rest I'm sure you can deduce for yourself."

"Oh."

"Sorry to disappoint. But I'm a magician. And we magicians have a certain tendency which ordinary mortals such as yourself do not."

"Which is?" said Flint.

Spector's smile became a grin. "We cheat."

ACKNOWLEDGEMENTS

T his seems like an ideal opportunity to highlight the work of the mystery writers who continue to enthuse and inspire me. Specifically: John Dickson Carr, Ellery Queen, Edward D. Hoch, Helen McCloy, Hake Talbot, Clayton Rawson, Nicholas Blake, and Christianna Brand, to name but a few. In addition, post–Golden Age masters such as Paul Halter and Soji Shimada have shown through continued innovation that the "impossible crime" still has a lot to offer.

I would like to thank *Ellery Queen's Mystery Magazine* and *Alfred Hitchcock's Mystery Magazine* for publishing some of the early Joseph Spector stories. Thanks also to everyone who read the stories and said nice things about them.

Thank you to Gabriele Crescenzi for his meticulous editorial feedback and keen eye for detail, as well as Rob Reef and Dan Napolitano for reading early drafts of the book.

Thanks to Michael Dahl and Ana Teresa Pereira for their friendship, encouragement, and continued enthusiasm for the Spector stories.

Thank you to Georgia Robinson, Milan Gurung, and Michael Pritchard. Last, thanks to Otto Penzler—for obvious reasons.

Read on for an excerpt from
Tom Mead's second Joseph Spector novel,

THE MURDER WHEEL

Coming soon from Mysterious Press

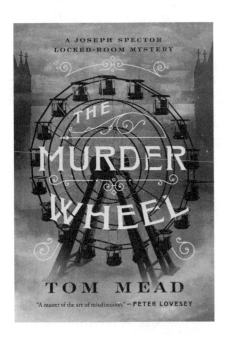

"A triple-barreled puzzle. . . . Even readers who
live to match wits with canny authors and detectives are
likely to be outwitted by this one."
—KIRKUS

"Brilliant . . . Mead plays scrupulously fair with his readers."
—PUBLISHERS WEEKLY (STARRED REVIEW)

CHAPTER ONE

"CAN *YOU* SOLVE THE FERRIS WHEEL MURDER CASE?"

I t began with the book. If not for the book, the rest of it would not have happened. At least, that's what Ibbs told himself after the fact. But truthfully, the whole hideous thing—every single facet of the case—slotted together so neatly that it was like an immaculately-timed sleight-of-hand trick. The quickness of the hand deceives the eye. But at the same time it had the kind of mad, surreal logic that is typically found in the most lucid and frenetic of fever dreams.

Ibbs did not believe in magic. And yet the macabre and bloody comedy of errors that occurred at the Pomegranate Theatre that night could not have unfurled more perfectly if it had been planned and executed by some invisible hellion. A puckish trickster, mocking his misfortune at every turn.

That was Friday, September 16, 1938: the day the gods played their wickedest trick on Edmund Ibbs.

But first: the book.

The morning began promisingly enough: a rap on the door of his quarters. He was lodging in upstairs rooms in Chancery Lane, not far from the Inns of Court in central London. Though he had not yet reached his thirtieth birthday, he'd completed his legal studies the previous summer and was now a full-fledged solicitor. Like all greenhorns, he was the object of his colleagues' blade-edged wit, and frequently found himself lumbered with heaps of the most tedious paperwork and monotonous administrative duties. But he didn't let it bother him. In fact, he considered it to be a rite of passage. No doubt they too had gone through it in their time, and now it was his turn.

At the door was the elderly porter Lancaster; stout and stolid as a pint of Guinness. He was holding a parcel.

"Morning Mr. Ibbs, sir."

"How do, Lancaster? Got something for me?"

"Book of some description, sir."

Ibbs took it, feeling its heft on his palm. He had scarcely said a cheery goodbye and closed the door again before he was wrenching the paper away. The scraps drifted lazily to the floor as he examined the book by the window. Its embossed title caught the light: *The Master of Manipulation.*

He could almost feel the book's talismanic power rippling through his fingers and up the length of his arms, like a tangible electrical charge. But it was just a book, he reminded himself.

Mere words on paper. What he was actually experiencing was an adrenaline surge; the excitement and anticipation bubbling over.

Ever since he first heard about *The Master of Manipulation*, Ibbs knew that he simply had to have a copy. It was not the sort of item a regular bookseller would stock, but he had a man in Marylebone who tracked down the more outré titles for him, and who had been only too willing to source a copy the day after it was published.

Though a lawyer by trade, Edmund Ibbs was also an enthusiastic amateur magician. Or, to use the appropriate term, *illusionist*. And when he first heard rumours of the book at a meeting of the London Occult Practice Collective (a trade organisation which was surprisingly welcoming when it came to amateurs) it had seemed like the answer to a prayer. Needless to say, the professionals were utterly scandalised. But for dilettantes like Ibbs, *The Master of Manipulation* was the book they had all been waiting for.

A magician lives and dies by the strength of his illusions. Drawing back the curtain to show the innermost workings of stage magic is a risk most conjurors would never take. There is an unspoken code concerning such things. But Ibbs was little more than a curious layman, and so the book (which was due to be published by a second-tier and not altogether reputable publishing house) was little short of a miracle. A single book containing a panoply of magical secrets—all the mysteries and wonders of the stage dispelled at a stroke!

The book was published under a foolish pseudonym—the sort of thing you'd usually find in the pages of *Punch*: Dr. Anne L.

Surazal. Ibbs had been puzzling over just who the wicked lady might be ever since he heard of the book's existence. It took an embarrassingly long time to spot that "Dr. Anne L. Surazal" is "Lazarus Lennard" spelled backward. But that information was little use without knowing who Lazarus Lennard might be. Some insider, perhaps, who knew the tricks of the trade.

Ibbs checked the clock on his mantle and judged he had enough time to get to grips with chapter one—which was tantalisingly titled "Cards from Nowhere"—before heading out into the damp and miserable September morning. He opened a drawer in his bureau and grabbed his own dog-eared Bicycle deck. He gave the cards a quick riffle shuffle and set them down on the table (a little messy, but all right otherwise). Then he focused on the text.

The frontispiece bore a minutely detailed pen-and-ink illustration of a Mephistophelean man (complete with goatee and curled moustache). He was one of the Acetabularii, history's first recorded illusionists; the cup-and-ball specialists of Ancient Rome. Ibbs was too excited to notice at the time, but a close examination of the drawing would have told him all he needed to know about how the cup-and-ball trick was done. You see, in the picture the conjuror is holding the ball between index finger and thumb of his right hand, presenting it to the observer. But look closely enough and you'll see reflected in the fellow's eyes the second ball, hidden from the audience in what's called a "Tenkai Palm," sandwiched between thumb and palm of his unobtrusive left hand. *The Master of Manipulation* was one of those books: all the answers were there if you knew how to look for them.

The art of magic, he read, *lies in the manipulation of perception. Most people will look exactly where you want them to; all you have to do is tell them. It is simply a matter of guiding their attention in the correct direction, so that they are never looking at the trick as it is being worked.*

Hardly earth-shattering, but it was enough to ensnare Ibbs's attention that morning, to the point where he was almost late for work. He soared through the first few chapters while eating a breakfast of porridge and dry toast, and it was with a heavy heart that he finally dragged himself away and readied himself to earn a day's pay. There was now the pesky business of the day job to be got out of the way. But it's safe to say that magic was at the forefront of his mind as he headed out to Holloway Prison that morning.

It was hard to leave the book behind, but Ibbs told himself that it would be much worse if he were to bring it with him and somehow lose it, or drop it in a puddle while shouldering his way through the rush-hour crowds. Instead he bought a newspaper from a seller on the corner, and boarded the omnibus. *The Master of Manipulation* would be waiting at his bedside when he got home.

It was difficult to concentrate on the tediously innuendo-laden headlines about Chamberlain's flight to Berchtesgaden and other such abstract political matters. The only flutter of interest he managed to muster was for a prize the *Chronicle* was offering:

CAN YOU SOLVE THE FERRIS WHEEL MURDER CASE?
THE DAILY CHRONICLE IS OFFERING A REWARD OF
TWO THOUSAND POUNDS TO ANYONE WHO
CAN DEMONSTRATE A SOLUTION TO
THE *IMPOSSIBLE* FERRIS WHEEL CRIME!

He folded the newspaper and slipped it under his arm with a sigh. At least the press was on his side. In the *Chronicle*, at least, she was innocent. But the court of public opinion and the court of law are two very different things.

While the omnibus trundled its way out to Parkhurst Road, his attention was caught by a boy of about six sitting across from him. The lad looked miserable and clung to his mother's skirts with palpable despondency. Ibbs took a coin out of his pocket, a sovereign. Then, very carefully as the bus traversed bumps and wove in and out of traffic, he began twirling the coin from knuckle to knuckle, showing off the practiced dexterity of his hands.

The boy watched for a little while, unsmiling and deathly serious. Ibbs placed the coin in the palm of his hand, snaring it in a tight fist. Then he held up two closed fists side by side, glancing at the boy expectantly. After some serious thought, the boy pointed to the right hand, the original hand which had held the coin. Ibbs spread his fingers, showing that the palm was empty. The coin had leapt to his other hand.

The boy's expression did not change, but Ibbs convinced himself there was a sparkle of enthusiasm in his eyes. Taking that as encouragement, he continued. He made the coin leap back and forth invisibly between his hands. It's a simple enough illusion, close in principle to the cup-and-ball trick. You just need another coin your audience doesn't know about. You always keep it just out of sight between the fingers of whichever hand is *not* flamboyantly demonstrating the trick. He had spent countless hours practicing in front of his mirror, just watching his reflection for the slightest hint of the second coin. If *he* couldn't see it, neither could his audience.

The coup de theatre: Ibbs lay flat both palms to show that they were empty. Then he clapped once, loudly enough to wake a woman sitting beside him from a snorting snooze. The boy watched in confusion. He looked up and down the bus to see if there was something he had missed. As he did so, the coin slipped from the dome of his young head and tumbled to the floor. Ibbs stretched out a leg and caught it on his shoe.

"That's yours," he said. The boy pounced on it and held it aloft as though it were some pirate's booty. Then he slipped it into the pocket of his shorts and got back to playing with his mother's skirts.

The next stop was Ibbs's. He stepped off the bus energised, if a sovereign lighter, and strode along Parkhurst Road toward the immense wooden gates of Holloway.

From the outside, Holloway Prison is a kind of palace of brown brick—immense and awe-inspiring, covering untold acres of land, but snared by high walls and discreetly razor-lined wire. A guard saluted as he stepped through the gate. Ibbs wasn't sure how to respond, so he saluted back. Then he kicked himself all the way up the path to the double doors—he should have simply looked at the fellow with steely disdain and then looked away. *That* is how a fellow commands respect.

An older uniformed man was waiting at the main entrance. "Ibbs?"

"That's me, sir."

"Very good. Warden Matthews." They shook hands. "You're here to see the 'lady of the moment,' I understand."

"Carla Dean."

"That's the one. Been keeping us busy, she has."

"Is she a troublesome prisoner then?"

"Not at all. Quiet as a mouse and very subdued. Reads her Bible a lot. But people are curious about her. Many's the time I've had to personally stop a reporter from sneaking in through our doors to try and snag an interview. They try all sorts of disguises. It can get quite comical."

"Seems counterintuitive to sneak into a prison," Ibbs observed.

Matthews laughed. "You're telling me."

The pair strode along drab corridors that reminded Ibbs eerily of his old boarding school. They shared that same conscious absence of ornament. Décor as a psychological weapon.

"You've visited Mrs. Dean before have you?"

"I met her once while she was in police custody. But that was with Sir Cecil. He did most of the talking."

"I see. And now they're trusting you to interview her solo?"

"Well, yes. Truth be told, we're all rather stretched." Ibbs had been roped in to assist the illustrious Sir Cecil Bullivant, QC, who would be acting for the defence. Bullivant had promptly come down with an acute case of copropraxia for which his bemused physician had prescribed bed rest. This left Ibbs with a considerable amount of work to do in the matter of the Crown versus Carla Dean. Currently, the case to be presented before Justice Sir Giles Drury was far from watertight.

The warden threw him a sideways smile: "Well, good luck."

What was that supposed to mean?

There was no denying the case had caused a sensation. Fleet Street christened its new baby the "Ferris Wheel Murder Case," which was an efficient summary of the key features. But the name did not convey the feeling of almost supernatural mystery which permeated the sequence of events. Two people went up on that Ferris wheel, and only one came down alive.

Ibbs had met Carla Dean once before, all too briefly. Not long enough to generate a lasting impression, at least. The newspaper photographs showed a young woman alive with intelligence and excitement. There was a glow about the face which seemed to seep from the photo paper. In prison she had aged decades. There were lines about her eyes and mouth that had grown shadowed, and her hair plumed messily. It was hard to believe this woman was not yet thirty. She wore a shapeless grey dress that looked to be fashioned out of sackcloth. Her thin, pianist's hands were threaded in her lap and she sat patiently, waiting for Ibbs to begin. Her eyes were deep; that is to say there was much in them he could not quite fathom. Like peering into twin chasms whose dimensions are beyond understanding. Like so much in this case, it only occurred to him after the fact, when he tried to picture Carla Dean again. But at that moment, as they faced each other across the cell, his only thought was how feeble he felt in her presence. How inadequate.

Did she look like a killer? It was a question which would need to be looked into seriously sooner or later. But there was undeniably something of the coiled spring in her knotted muscles and the feline uprightness with which she perched on the bed. The stillness too; the stillness meant something. . . .

To be continued in

THE MURDER WHEEL